The Adventures of Auggie Thumb
J.A. Hester

Turtle Bay Press, LLC

This is a work of fiction. The characters, incidents, and dialogues are products of the author's imagination and are not to be construed as real. Any resemblance to actual events or persons, living or dead, is coincidental.

Copyright © 2024 by J.A. Hester

Illustrations by Marianne Constable, Copyright © 2024 by J.A. Hester

All rights reserved. No part of this book, or the characters within it, may be used or reproduced in any manner whatsoever without written permission from the publisher or author, except in the case of brief quotations embodied in critical articles and reviews.

The Library of Congress has cataloged the paperback edition of this work. (Library of Congress Control Number: 2024905090)

ISBN 978-0-9789388-3-3 (paperback) | ISBN 978-0-9789388-4-0 (eBook)

Published in the United States by Turtle Bay Press, LLC, South Hero, Vermont

Chapter One

The Amazing Houdini

Iowa, 1971

It was a sticky hot July day. The kind of day where your blue jeans stick to your legs and discomfort was the best comfort for which you could hope. On that day, none of us had any energy, and heavy sighing was all we could muster as we tried to think of what to do. We sat on the lawn in the shade with our backs against the side of the house where the concrete blocks below the siding felt cool to the touch.

"Whaddya guys wanna do?" I asked no one in particular. "I'm bored."

"Quit whining Auggie," my older brother Timmy replied.

"You guys should shut up!" my other brother David said. Then he added, "It's too hot to do anything, and besides, there's nothing to do."

I'm eleven and my name is August Maxwell Thumb. My brothers, Timmy and David, are twins and are almost exactly two years older than me. Our parents missed it by one day. I was born on December 14th and they were born two years before me on December 15th. Timmy is the oldest by one and a half minutes, but David is the biggest, and he doesn't let us forget it. Mom said that they really wanted to name the first boy Thomas after her dad, but just couldn't bring themselves to name a child "Tom Thumb." So they went with Timothy, however, when everyone shortened it to Tim – which being too close to Tom – annoyed my parents, they reluctantly allowed him to be called Timmy. They told us that they didn't like boy names that ended in the "E" sound like Timmy, Jimmy, Tommy, etc... however, since they didn't want to go with Tim, and no one other than them would call him Timothy, Timmy it was. For the second twin to come into this world they chose the name David. They didn't think anyone would try to turn David into Davy since the only one that could really pull off Davy was the famous Colonel Crockett, and no one would try that, him being the hero of the Alamo and all.

When I came to be, my parents thought that they had the ultimate non-E sounding name and called me "August" which my uncle Kenny, much to my Mom's chagrin, promptly shortened to "Auggie." It stuck, and now I'm an Auggie.

Being eleven with two thirteen-year-old brothers isn't as glamorous as you might at first think. Actually, it's as unbearable as you might at first think. Timmy and David would mostly get along, but Timmy being smarter (well at least he thought he was) and David being bigger (he actually was) could lead to some good arguments and fights. In spite of this, the one thing that they did agree on and didn't fight over was that an eleven-year-old brother who was two years younger than they were was a good thing to pick on, and when it was a hot muggy summer day with nothing to do, what could be better than picking on him. 'Him' in this case, was me.

Now on any summer day there was no real good reason to be inside after breakfast even if we were stuck in the middle of Iowa in the middle of July. If we were outside, there was always the possibility of coming up with a plan that could lead to an adventure. As it was, if we were inside we'd either get roped into doing chores or told to read books, and what fun would that be? We'd be reading soon enough when school started in about six weeks. It was better to just hang out in the backyard and try to think of something to do.

On this particular day, Dad was working downtown in his office, and Mom had gone to lunch with some of her friends. It's not as if she'd left us on our own, our older sister Polly was home. Mom and Dad liked "E" sounding names for girls and that's why they named her Polly. Polly was sixteen and as such was deemed responsible. Polly however wanted nothing to do with us. She shooed us outside the moment Mom left for lunch with Mrs. Harris and Mrs. Mahoney.

Whenever Mom had to go somewhere during the day, either Dad would take the bus downtown to his office, or Mom would drive him in the morning so that she could keep the car since we only had one, and it was an old station wagon.

With Mom gone, as soon as we were outside, Polly jumped on the phone to talk with one of her friends. If Mom and Dad weren't home, Polly would spend hours on our phone talking with her friends. We only had one phone mounted on the wall in the kitchen and its cord was just long enough to allow you to sit in the chair directly below the phone when you were talking, so if anyone else was in the kitchen, there was no such thing as a private conversation.

To us it was no big deal. The only person that I'd ever call was my best friend Dean Nolan. Dean lived catty-corner across the street from us and was six months older than me. And if I called him, it was just to see if he wanted to come over, or go do something. Most of the time I just ran across the street to his house and knocked on their door, since that took about the same amount of time as it did to dial his number. So, no big deal, the phone for me. However, for our sister, that phone was her lifeline to the outside world. I never could figure out how sixteen-year-old girls could talk so much and say so little. I think that it had something to do with being in high school. I mean, as soon as she was on the phone, anyone that tried to call our house for the rest of that day got nothing but a busy signal. I swear, if the phone company only had one busy signal, Polly owned it.

"Hey Timmy," David said all casual like. "Do you remember that magician guy who could escape from being tied up, what was his name? Houdini, right?"

"Yeah, it was Houdini, whyd-jah ask?"

"Cuz I bet you can't escape if I tie your hands up," David replied.

I wasn't quick enough to see the wink from David to Timmy, so I had no idea that when this was all said and done, it wouldn't be ending well for me.

"I bet I can," said Timmy.

"Isn't there some old clothesline in the basement by Dad's workbench?" David asked.

"Yeah there is, and I know right where it is!" I blurted out before Timmy could even answer.

As the words left my mouth I enthusiastically jumped up and volunteered to go get it.

"Auggie, that'd be great if you'd fetch it for us, and then we'll see just how much of a Houdini Timmy really is."

I jumped up like a grasshopper who had springs for feet, and ran for the back door. Now that I had a mission to accomplish, and I was included in my brothers' game, I was all full of energy. I bounded up the three steps of the back door's stoop, pulled open the screen door, two steps to the basement door, pulled that open and bounded down the basement stairs. At the bottom of the stairs, it was a quick left turn to the wooden crate full of old hand tools, bits of wood and other odds and ends next to Dad's workbench. I knelt down on the floor beside the crate and hurriedly fished out the coil of clothesline rope. All of that in reverse order, and I was back outside in a jiffy.

Timmy and David had moved into the garage. We had a single car garage that set back a bit from our house and with the door all the way up, even on a day as hot as this, it was cool enough for practicing escape tricks. Timmy was sitting on a wooden box turned on its side and David was standing next to him. I handed David the rope and he told Timmy to hold out his hands. Timmy did, and then David tied a big knot on his right wrist, wrapped the rope around his left wrist, then back and forth under and over his wrists in a figure-8 motion until it looked to me like there was no way Timmy would ever be able to get out of it.

"All right, let's see if you can escape out of that," David said to Timmy.

"Timmy, you're never gonna be able to untie that! David's really got you hog-tied!" I said.

It felt like David and I were against Timmy, and it felt good to be on the side of two instead of the odd man out, like I usually was.

"Okay start when I say go, and you have to get out in less than two minutes like Houdini did, and remember he was wrapped in chains and stuck in a box underwater," David told Timmy.

"Go," shouted David, with me echoing it a split-second later.

Timmy started wriggling and struggling as David watched the second hand on his wristwatch move steadily around the dial. With a bit of huffing and puffing in full concentration with the tip of his tongue sticking out between his lips, Timmy bent and contorted his wrists trying to grab the rope with his fingers. He was failing miserably, and I loved every last second of it! My smartest oldest brother was not going to get out and I was the one who had gotten the rope for this trick. But then, with less than 20 seconds to spare, Timmy brought his hands up to his mouth, grasped the rope with his teeth, and pulled an end free from the outermost loop of the knot. After that, he was able to create enough slack to get one wrist free, and then just like that, he was out and it was over. He was just as good as Houdini!

"That was too easy!" I shouted.

"Maybe you think that you can do better?" Timmy asked me.

"Yeah, I can easily get out of being tied up," I replied, the words coming out quicker than I could think.

"Well, you already saw how I did it with just my hands tied, so to make it fair, we're going to tie up your feet as well as your hands."

And at that, Timmy tied my hands while David tied my feet together. Then for good measure David pulled me over to the inside wall of the garage and looped the end of the rope around the two-by-four that Dad had nailed across the studs about three feet up from the floor to hold all his shovels and rakes and stuff between the studs along the side of the garage.

"Why you tyin' me to the wall?" I asked.

"We don't want you to have an unfair advantage," David answered.

I was surely hog-tied and couldn't really move very much, so I didn't see what unfair advantage I might have.

"Okay, start the timer," I said.

I was full of myself on this and thought that I could get out of it in no time.

"We will," said Timmy.

And with that, they both stepped out of the garage, but not before pulling the door down and sealing me inside.

"Hey!" I shouted. "Get back here!"

I couldn't believe how stupid I'd been. Not only had I volunteered to be tied up, I'd gone and fetched the rope for them to tie me up with! I brought my hands up to my mouth to use my teeth to work a knot loose, but it didn't budge one dang bit. There was no way I was getting free that way. Since they'd tied me to the wall there was no way I could worm my way over to the garage door, and even if I did, I wouldn't be able to lift up the door. I was really in a pickle. I hollered to try to get Polly's attention, but with her ear stuck to the phone receiver in the house, she wasn't going to hear me unless I lit off fireworks.

Now, I wasn't bored, and I surely had something to do, but this wasn't what I had in mind when I told Timmy and David that I was bored earlier. Sitting there against the garage wall all tied up, I figured that the earliest I was getting out of there would be when Mom got home from lunch – and by my best guess, that would be at least another two hours!

After what seemed like an eternity but was more likely just five or ten minutes, the garage door slowly rolled up, and with David holding it up over his head, there stood my two brothers

grinning from ear to ear and shaking their heads laughing at me.

"You guys stink!" I shouted. "That's a rotten trick!"

"Oh come on, don't be a sore loser, you're fine," Timmy said.

Then, just to put it all into perspective, David added, "It's not like you were in chains, stuck in a box, underwater or anything!"

After some more hemming and hawing and teasing, they finally untied me. Rubbing my wrists, I got up off the floor of the garage and we all went out to the backyard and sat on the grass in the shade with our backs against the side of the house where the concrete blocks below the siding felt cool to the touch.

Chapter Two

THE ROBINSONS

O'MALLEY PARK WAS A little over a mile from our house. It was at the end of a dead-end road and consisted of a sandlot baseball field with a chain link backstop, a jungle gym and about two acres of open space. While it was only a mile or so away, it was across 32nd street, which is the busy road that separated our neighborhood from the O'Malley Park neighborhood so we really didn't go over there much. Another reason that we didn't go over there much was the

Robinson brothers. Everyone said that fourteen-year-old Billy Robinson was the toughest kid in town. He had three younger brothers, Robby, Wes, and Donny who were just as tough as Billy, and supposedly they claimed O'Malley Park as their turf, so going over there was risking life and limb. All that being said, I'd only seen Billy Robinson once and that was last summer at the state fair when he was with his family and I was with mine, so nothing happened. Heck, I never woulda even known who it was if Timmy hadn't pointed him out to me. However, it being summer, it being hot, and it being Iowa, we needed to do something different. Timmy had heard that the Robinsons were out of town, so that day we told Mom that we were going to ride over to O'Malley Park and play some baseball. Timmy, David, and I got our gloves, a ball, and a bat and with our gloves pulled over our handlebars, and Timmy holding the ball in one hand and David holding the bat across his handlebars, we set off for the park.

It was an easy pedal to get there as the whole area is pretty flat. As far as bikes go, we had a mixed bag of cycling technology. Timmy and David both had Schwinn bikes that had been handed down from our cousins, Uncle Kenny's kids. Timmy had a blue three speed that he could ride no-hands like a pro, and David a brown five speed that was the fastest of the lot. Since Uncle Kenny and Aunt Lorraine only had two boys there were only two bikes to hand down, so for my tenth birthday Mom and Dad had gotten me a five speed green Schwinn Stingray with the high handlebars, and the gearshift right in front of the banana seat. Depending on what gear you were in, if you had to slam on the brakes to make a sudden stop you could end up singing soprano for at least a week if you weren't careful. However, as far as I was concerned, the Stingray was the coolest bike out there.

On our ride to O'Malley Park, we had to be careful and ride single file on 32nd Street, but only for two blocks until we turned onto Maple Drive and could once more ride all together. It was about ten o'clock in the morning when we got to the park. No one else was there so we had the place to ourselves. Timmy called being up first and David called pitching, so I was stuck in the outfield shagging the ball. With only one ball, I had to be quick.

"Come on Timmy, let's see whatcha got!" I yelled.

Without a catcher, if the batter missed, he had to go pick up the ball from wherever it stopped rolling and then throw it back to the pitcher, so this wasn't really major league batting practice or anything. However, while my brothers could do it without a catcher, they couldn't do it without a fielder, so I got to be included!

After a couple of pitches, swings and misses Timmy finally hit one out. I ran after it and just barely caught it, but catch it I did and I was thrilled to be able to throw it to David. Our rule was to change if the batter hit it into the outfield, and since Timmy did, it was now David's turn to bat. Neither one of them ever wanted me to pitch to them, nor can I say that I blame them, as both of them were better pitchers than me.

Timmy wound up a good fastball and sent it screaming across the plate, but David was all over it and with a mighty swing, he smacked it solidly, sending it deep into the outfield way over my head. Turning around I ran like heck for the ball.

It was a great hit, and without an outfield fence I had to get the ball before it rolled down the hill behind the outfield.

As soon as I started to run after the ball, that's when I saw them – the Robinson brothers. They'd just come up over the hill behind the outfield and that's why we hadn't seen them. We didn't know where they lived, but we knew that they considered this their park and their neighborhood. Clearly they weren't out of town like Timmy thought. They didn't go to the same school as us, and frankly, we didn't know if they even went to school. I really wanted to turn and run back to Timmy and David, but we only had the one ball and if I went back to my brothers, we wouldn't have a baseball at all, so I continued running towards the ball.

The ball hit the ground, bounced, and rolled up to where the Robinson boys were standing. Billy, being the oldest and biggest, picked up the ball and held it out in front of him like he was admiring a brand-new trophy. I gulped. I was caught out in the open surrounded by all four Robinsons and my brothers were way at the other end of the field. Even though I was frozen in fear, my mouth still worked, and without engaging my brain I said,

"Hey, that's my ball!"

"Are you sure this is yours? I mean I just found it." Billy replied.

Billy had a slight smile on his face when he spoke so I couldn't tell if he was being friendly or just sizing me up the way a bulldog sizes up a steak. Knowing that he could squash me like a bug made me realize that I had nothing to lose, so I put a smile on my face and said,

"Ya know, I've been shagging balls for my brothers for about half an hour and I could really use some help if you guys want to join us."

"Billy slowly lowered his hand holding our baseball, looked over at his brothers and said,

"So whadda you guys wanna do? You wanna show these guys who rules this park?"

"Absolutely Billy, that'd be fun!" said one of his brothers.

I was petrified! I had no idea what they considered to be the fun way to show intruders who ruled the park! I just imagined Billy pounding me into the ground like a tent stake while his brothers went after David and Timmy. I was almost ready to run when Billy turned back to me and with a slight nod of his head said, "Okay, you're on, Squirt!"

When he tossed our ball back to me I saw that he and his brothers had all their baseball stuff as well, so baseball was going to be how we determined who ruled the park.

Just then my brothers came running up behind me. David held the bat loosely in his right hand and I wasn't sure what thoughts were going through his head, but I think that they were all set to defend me. However, before they could say or do anything, Billy came up to David and said, "My name's Billy, what's yours?"

David's mouth just dropped open and he started stammering and stuttering for words, but after a few seconds he finally remembered who he was and said,

"I'm David, um, yeah, yeah I'm David."

Billy looked at him and more than likely was thinking that David might not be all right in the head or something, and said,

"Good to meet you, David. These guys are all my brothers, and if you don't mind, we're gonna whup you guys in baseball!"

At that we all introduced ourselves to each other and the seven of us headed back to the field.

"What kind of name is Auggie?" Wes asked me as we shuffled back to the diamond.

"It's a long story." I answered.

"Just call him Squirt," Billy told his brother.

When we got back to the diamond, we spread out in the infield and outfield and all took turns batting and pitching. Billy by far was the best pitcher, but David managed to get a hit off of him. We played for about another hour or so until it was just too hot with the midday sun blazing down on us.

"I think I'm melting. I'm gonna find some shade." Timmy said to no one in particular.

"Sounds like a good idea," Robby answered.

We all headed over to where we'd parked our bikes and sat down under the trees. Sitting in the shade we talked about baseball and summer stuff and after a few minutes David said, "We'd better be taking off."

"Yeah, we've gotta get home too," Billy answered. "Just so ya know, we live in that big yellow house over there," Billy added as he pointed across the field. "Our backyard backs up to the park and our dad put a gate in our fence so it's super easy to get over here. Next time you guys come over to the park, just knock on our back door and if we're around we can play ball again."

I couldn't believe what I was hearing. Here was supposedly the toughest guy in town inviting us to come play baseball with him and his brothers anytime!

"That sounds great." David answered.

"Hey, Squirt, you can come too." Billy laughed.

"It's Auggie," I said.

"Okay, Squirt, whatever you say!"

Uggh, clearly Billy had no intention of ever calling me Auggie.

As the Robinson brothers headed off to their house, we got on our bikes and started riding away from the park. As we pedaled home, I couldn't help but think back to when Timmy and David had come running up to me when I was trying to get our ball back from Billy.

"Hey David, when I was out there with Billy and his brothers, and you guys came running up to me, were you coming up to rescue me or something? I mean, I saw you with the bat and everything. I can't believe that you and Timmy were ready to fight Billy Robinson to protect me!"

David stopped pedaling and coasted his bike alongside Timmy till they both slowed to a stop. I stopped too. He stood there straddling his bike, looked over at Timmy and then turned to face me. As he did so, he reached out and grabbed my handlebars.

"Look, Squirt," he said, using the same nickname that Billy Robinson had called me. "Don't go thinking that we did it to stop you from getting a beating, that wasn't the reason at all, we did it because we're the only ones that are allowed to beat you. Got it, *Squirt*?

"Yeah, I got it." I answered.

I didn't feel like pushing it any further, and besides, other than the new nickname that I didn't really appreciate, at that moment, knowing that they were ready to fight to protect me, I knew that my brothers really did love me.

Chapter Three

Catch me if you can

A FTER THE DAY AT O'Malley Park, we decided to do something different. Mom had to run a bunch of errands, so once again she left Polly in charge. However, before she left she gave us a whole list of chores to do and, as always, she told us to behave. Needless to say, with a pile of chores in front of us, none of us were in the best of moods, but for some reason Timmy and David seemed extra grumpy. After we finished our chores, Polly made a beeline for the phone and I plopped down in the living room to watch some TV.

I had just found the show I wanted to watch, it wasn't that hard as there were only three channels, not counting the public channel, which no one in their right mind would watch unless he had a hankering for bad puppet shows, learning how to knit, or people in thick glasses with wide neckties talking about planting radishes, electing mayors or some other such nonsense. Now our TV wasn't one of those fancy new expensive ones that had all the shows in color, ours was an old black and white, and the only way to get the picture to be somewhat clear was to prop the channel selector knob into position with a wooden stick, which Dad had cut to fit under the knob.

I finally got the picture on the TV to be good enough to watch, with the stick moved into position to hold the selector knob just so, when David walked into the living room.

"Whaddya watching, Squirt?"

My brothers had come to really enjoy calling me "Squirt" but considering all the other things that they could've called me, and the fact that I had no say in the matter, I'd come to begrudgingly accept it.

"Nothing," I responded.

"Well in that case, let's see what else is on," David said as he pulled the stick away from the channel knob and started to turn it to one of the other two channels.

"Hey!" I yelled. "I was watching that!"

"Tough!"

At that, I grabbed him and started to wrestle him away from the TV. In our family, we had rules about fighting. Wrestling was okay, and so was hitting, but only in the shoulder, leg or stomach. You couldn't punch in the face, nor could you hit anyone with anything other than your hands – weapons were absolutely forbidden.

Obviously I was losing badly against David, and he seemed to be taking extra enjoyment in holding me down and turning the TV dial between the channels, purposely passing over the show I had been trying to watch and landing instead on the others. Just to make it worse he kept it on the public channel. I finally wriggled free but with him blocking my access to the TV, I couldn't do anything. All my frustration and anger welled up inside of me and forgetting our house fighting rules, I picked up the wooden TV stick and smacked him straight on the shin!

Oh boy, was that a mistake! David grabbed his shin and howled in anger and pain. Knowing that if I hung around an instant longer I'd get a right royal beating, I turned and sprinted down the hall to the only room in our house that had a locking door, our bathroom. David was hot on my heels, but I was able to shove the door shut and lock it before he could push it open.

"I'm gonna kill you!" he bellowed at me from the other side of the door.

"David, I'm sorry," I said, none too convincingly from the safety of the bathroom.

"Yeah, well that ain't gonna save you!"

We were in a standoff. If I opened that door, I was a dead man. However, he couldn't break the door down, because with a broken bathroom door when Dad got home, he'd be a dead man. So there we were, me dejectedly sitting on the toilet and David angrily leaning against the wall right outside of the bathroom door. Suddenly David tried a new approach.

"Auggie, just open the door and we can talk about this, I promise that I won't hurt you."

Yeah right, I thought. I had eleven years' experience living with my brothers, and while I might do a lot of stupid things, I wasn't that much of a fool.

"Forget it Dave," I yelled through the closed door. "I'm not falling for that!"

I could hear David muttering as he stood in the hallway.

Now the only thing that was going to save me was Mom coming home, and I had no idea when that'd be. As it was, I no more wanted to sit stuck in a bathroom on a beautiful summer day than David wanted to lurk in a hallway waiting to pound me, so we were both in a pickle. Sitting there in the bathroom, I looked up at the window and an idea crossed my mind. The window was partially open to let in the breeze. I figured that if I pushed it all the way up, I could fit through the bottom of it. All I needed to do was pop out the screen. As quiet as the proverbial church mouse, I loosened the two tabs on the bottom of the screen and pulled it away from the house. It was only about four feet off the ground, so once I had it free from the house, I let the screen fall onto the grass. The window was right above the bathtub, so I stepped onto the side of the tub, stuck my head and shoulders out the window, braced my hands against the outside wall, and with a mighty kick I pushed myself out and onto the grass.

I was free! Now what? I decided that I'd just head over to the Nolan's and see my best friend Dean. As I started to jog over there, I thought of my dopey older brother still waiting in the hallway ready to pounce like a lion that has a gazelle pinned in a hollow, and I couldn't resist. I crept all ninja-like up to the back door, opened it without the slightest noise, and tiptoed into the living room. I looked down the hallway to the closed bathroom door and sure enough, there was David poised in strike mode against the wall just outside of it. Yep, he was all lion-like and I would've been dead gazelle meat if I'd opened that door. Rather than retreating quietly and letting it lay, I threw caution to the wind and shouted at him,

"Hey idiot, whaddya doing?"

He spun around with the most confused look on his face, but I spun even faster, and with my Red Ball Jets burning out on the living room carpet, I flew out the back door, leapt over all three steps of the concrete stoop, hit the driveway at full speed, and with nary a second thought, sprinted over to the Nolan's house as if my life depended on it, which in this case, it actually did!

David was in hot pursuit. He was bigger and faster than me, but I had a head start and knew where I was going. Unfortunately, he was quickly gaining on me. I rounded the corner of the hedge that ran around the perimeter of the Nolan's backyard with my feet fairly well flying out from under me and in four quick steps I was at the sliding glass door on the back of their house. Just as my hand hit the doorframe in a frantic knock, David's hand came down on my shoulder in the most crushing vise-like grip he could muster.

"Well hello boys," Mrs. Nolan said from inside their house. She was sitting at the kitchen table enjoying a cup of coffee, reading the morning paper, and with only the screen door between her and us, she was able to see and hear everything that was happening right there on her back patio.

"Sorry, but Dean isn't here right now, he had to go run an errand with his father," she said as she set her paper down.

My hear sank. David's however, soared.

"That's okay, Mrs. Nolan, my mom's not home and I was wondering if I could talk to you and pet Jangles," I said.

The Nolan's had a cute little poodle named Jangles, and with us not having a dog, Jangles was our default dog, and at this particular moment, that dog was my emergency lifeline.

"Well okay, Auggie, I guess that's fine."

"David, would you like to come in as well?" Mrs. Nolan asked.

"No thank you, Mrs. Nolan, I think I'll go back home and wait."

He answered her just dripping with pleasantness, but the look he shot at me told me that this was far from over.

A huge sigh of relief escaped out of me. I didn't care, I could hang out here at the Nolan's until my brother cooled down, and hopefully all would return to normal. In the meantime, I got to play with Jangles and not only that, but dang it all if Mrs. Nolan didn't find a plateful of chocolate chip cookies to feed me!

Chapter Four

THE CRICK

WHEN DEAN CAME HOME, he wasn't a bit surprised to see me in his kitchen, as I was over there as much as he was over at my house. Dean was big for his age. He was even a bit bigger than David was and him being closest to me in age was more my friend than Timmy and David's, but they liked hanging out with him and we all got along real well. Knowing that, and knowing that David probably wouldn't start pounding me in front of Dean, I invited him to come over to our house and help us figure out what we could do that day. Four brains being better than three.

When we got to our house, Timmy and David were outside sitting on the back stoop as it was now in the shade. Dean plopped down on the bottom step and leaned against the side of the house. I sat on the ground next to Dean. Mom had come home, which meant that Polly had to get off the phone to allow it to cool down to room temperature. David still nursed a grudge against me, but with Dean sitting with us and Mom home, I wasn't in any imminent danger. Now I just had to figure out how to get my upcoming beating out of David's mind. Rather than wait for the round of "Whaddya want to do now" questions, I suggested going to the crick.

"Do you guys want to go to the crick?" I asked.

Now the crick, or creek, as my third grade teacher Mrs. Gruetzmacher always corrected us when she heard us say "crick," was about a half mile from our house in the opposite direction from O'Malley Park so it was technically still in our neighborhood, but that was stretching the boundaries of our neighborhood a might bit. As a waterway, it wasn't much. At most places you could jump across it and it was only a few inches deep. However, the exception was when it rained. We rarely got to see it during a big thunderstorm when it'd be completely swollen and running in its full majesty, since as a general rule Mom didn't want us playing outside during thunderstorms, but at its peak it could be several feet deep and eight or ten feet across. As quickly as it would swell up to that level, it would subside once all the run-off had gone by and flowed into a bigger brook which eventually drained into the river several miles downstream. However, after a night's rain, even hours later, it would still be running deeper and faster than normal, and last night it'd rained quite a bit, so it was a perfect time to go down there.

"Yeah, let's do that," Dean said.

Once Dean had agreed with something then my brothers would be more eager to join in since as soon as Dean agreed, it ceased being my idea.

We told Mom that we were going to the crick and she told us to be careful. If we were going to a park or someone else's house, we were always told to "behave." If we were going to do something more outdoorsy or that required a bit of exploring or woodsmanship, we were always told to "be careful." Since it was the crick, careful was the guidance Mom gave.

We rode our bikes over to Dean's, he got his mom's permission and his bike, and away we rode down the hill towards our white-water adventure.

Now the crick wound its way between the backyards of the houses on Hawthorne Drive on one side and the backyards of the houses on Elm Street on the other until it crossed under Beechwood Drive, ran out into a wooded area and then into the other larger brook. We weren't headed to that one as it was a lot further away and required more planning, we were just going down to the bottom of our street where we'd park our bikes on the sidewalk and climb down to where the crick ran through a culvert under the road.

The culvert was a round concrete pipe that formed a tunnel six feet in diameter and about thirty feet long. At each end of it were vertical concrete sides that stretched from the bottom of the crick bed about eight feet up to the sidewalk. These sides were about ten inches thick and three feet wide, flared out from the tunnel openings and funneled the water into and out of the culvert during storms so our road above it wouldn't flood.

We got off our bikes and peered over the railing that ran along the sidewalk and saw about six or seven inches of water flowing through the bottom of the culvert. We were at the downstream end, and right in front of the culvert's opening the crick was about four feet wide and at least a foot deep. At that depth, the stream running through the bottom of the culvert was about two feet wide. We scrambled down the bank and tried to see if we could get into the culvert without getting our shoes wet.

"Who's going first?" I asked.

We all wanted to go into the culvert because it was cooler in there and once you were in, the echoes made it fun to shout things out.

"I'll go," said David.

He wasn't going to let his little brother beat him to it, so with one big angled leap he jumped across the stream and into the culvert. His right foot landed perfectly above the water line on the far side of the stream, and as his left foot came down it just barely missed the water, so he was cleanly in with dry feet. Once he had his feet under him he stood part way up on the curved side of the pipe. He couldn't walk on the bottom because of the water, so he kept his knees bent and leaned into the side to keep from sliding down into the water.

Next, it was Timmy's turn and instead of trying to jump the crick, he turned, placed his right hand against the inside of the pipe, and staying on the same side of the stream that we were on outside the culvert's mouth, he attempted to step into the pipe with his right foot while holding onto the outer lip of the pipe with his left hand. I don't know if he'd seen someone do something like that in a movie or something, but once he was committed to the pipe and in motion, he had nowhere to put his left foot and when he tried to bring it under him, his right foot slid straight down the side of the pipe and right into the water. However, he'd gotten in, but now he had one wet foot and one dry foot.

Dean started laughing at Timmy and said to him, "Hey, Thumb that was a cool move!"

"Yeah, it was supposed to work better than it did," Timmy answered.

Dean was next, he followed the method that David had used and he made it successfully as well. Now it was my turn. I had seen how Timmy's method wasn't that smart, but I also saw how far I had to jump to copy David and Dean so I wasn't sure what I was going to do.

"Jump Squirt!" David yelled at me.

He loved using that name, and I think that he wanted to do it in front of Dean to show off a bit. Dean however didn't let on that he heard David call me Squirt, and instead he said encouragingly,

"Come on Auggie, you can do it."

So, just like an Olympic hurdler, I gave a mighty leap, clearly visualizing my landing clean and dry on the other side. Unfortunately, the splash of my right Red Ball Jet landing squarely in the middle of the crick wiped all Olympic glory from my mind, and just to make sure it was completely gone, the sound of my left foot hitting the water made it official. My feet were soaked.

Now that we were in the pipe, we could run up and down alongside the stream and easily jump from side to side. We all went to the upstream end and looked at the pool of water that had formed there as it drained into the pipe. This was the best place to be because even when the crick was at its lowest, this part of it always had at least several inches of water in it. Today it was about two feet deep and we were looking for crawdads, frogs, minnows, whatever we could find.

We'd brought two cardboard milk cartons with us so that we could keep our catch in case we found some good specimens. Minnows were hard to catch without a net, and if frogs saw you coming they were gone in a flash, however what we really wanted were crawdads. In case you don't know, crawdads look like little lobsters, and some of the big ones can give you quite a pinch with their claws. However, they were the most fun and made great bait for bass fishing. If we got enough of them, then Dad would take us to McDevitt's Pond to go fishing.

Chapter Five

Crawdads

C RAWDADS HIDE IN THE water under rocks or plants, usually along the edges of the stream. So in order to catch them, you have to lift up the rock with one hand and be ready to grab it with your other hand before it scoots away. If you're not careful, they can pinch your finger with their claws, but it doesn't really hurt, and even if it did, I'd never let on. Actually, they look more frightening than they really are.

We jumped out of the pipe and onto the bank on the upstream side of the culvert, and getting out of the pipe was a lot easier than getting into it. However, with both of my shoes soaking wet, it didn't really matter to me. We spread out and started hunting along the edge of the water. Dean and Timmy had been the first two out of the pipe and they were on the left side of the crick. David and I jumped out onto the bank opposite them so that we could cover both sides and we weren't all bunched up fighting to see who could find the best crawdad hiding places.

I was ahead of David and moved alongside the stream with my eyes glued to the water's edge trying to find the good crawdad hiding places. Suddenly I came upon this fist-sized rock that if you were a crawdad would be the most perfect place to hang out.

"David, check this one out."

"Yep, that looks like a good place for one to be hiding, Auggie."

The crawdad hunting seemed like it'd removed all his feelings of getting me back for whacking him with the stick.

"You lift the rock, real slow like and I'll try to grab him," he added.

Now when you're catching crawdads with your hands, you gotta pay real close attention to which way the stream is flowing, cuz how you lift the rock determines whether or not the crawdad stays put or gets away. You always want to lift the rock and gently turn it so that its bottom is facing upstream and that way any sediment or mud that gets stirred up won't block your view since it'll move with the current downstream. If you lift the rock too fast, you'll scare the crawdad and it'll scoot right out of there.

I got myself into position, bent down and slid my hand around the rock. I very carefully worked my fingertips under the edges of it, and once the rock was well in my hand, I slowly raised and tilted it. A little bit of mud came free, which formed a tiny cloud in the water but after a second or two, it drifted away downstream. David was on the upstream side of me, and I could tell by the look in his eye that it was a good-sized crawdad. With great determination, he angled his hand so that it was right above and behind it, then ever so slowly he moved his hand from the crawdad's back to its front, and using his thumb and index finger, he grabbed it right behind its claws.

"Wow, look at that one!" I hollered. "That's a beaut! Man, oh man, David, we're gonna catch a monster bass with that one!" I added.

We dropped it in the milk carton and kept on looking for more.

Timmy and Dean had similar luck on the other side and all in all, after about an hour of hunting, we had eleven crawdads. We had also gotten real lucky and caught several minnows. Dean had found a small school of them trapped in a little pool with no way out. Once the run-off had receded the pool was closed off from the rest of the stream and the minnows didn't really have a way back into it. We scooped them out with the milk carton.

With our amazing catch of bait, instead of trying to get back into the culvert and go under the street, we just climbed up the bank and popped out on the opposite side of the street from where we'd parked our bikes.

Dean and David each held a milk carton and we all got on our bikes for the pedal home. Thinking about all the bass that we'd catch at McDevitt's Pond made me forget all about my soggy sneakers.

We had to wait until 5:30 that evening before Dad got home to see if he could take us fishing. While we waited we put the milk cartons with our amazing haul of crawdads and minnows in our backyard up against the wall of the house in the shade to keep them cool. Otherwise, the summer sun would boil 'em alive.

Since Mom had kept the car that day, Dad had taken the bus. The bus stop was about a block from our house, and I was waiting for him when the bus pulled up. I liked walking home with Dad from the bus stop because he always asked what I'd done that day, and it gave me time to talk with him before he got home and became surrounded with everything else going on.

He stepped off the bus and started towards me.

"Hi ya Auggie!" He shouted.

He had a grin on his face when he saw me and I ran up and gave him a hug.

"Hi Dad!"

Before he could respond, I immediately asked him, "Hey can you take us fishing at McDevitt's Pond tonight right after supper?"

Instead of responding with an enthusiastic "absolutely my boy" Dad took a deep breath, tilted his head, and let out a sigh.

Clearly he was getting ready to tell me something that I wasn't going to like.

"I don't think so Auggie, Mr. Hoffman asked if I could help him move some furniture when I got home, so unfortunately there won't be enough time tonight."

"What about tomorrow night?" I asked.

"Well, tomorrow night we're all going over to Howard and Mary's for supper, so it'll have to be Saturday morning."

"Saturday morning! They'll all be dead by then!" I wailed.

"What'll all be dead by then?" Dad asked.

"All the crawdads and minnows we caught down at the crick today," I explained.

"Oh, I see," said Dad.

"You'll just have to find some place to put them so that they'll keep. Hopefully, they'll still be good by Saturday."

Kicking at a rock on the sidewalk I couldn't hide my disappointment. I was really hoping that we could all go fishing tonight. I'd just been too eager and before I blurted out the question, I should've first warmed him up a bit by asking him how his day went, or how his bus ride was, or something like that, but it'd be a few years before I got to be that smart.

Uggh, I couldn't believe that we weren't going to be able to go fishing. McDevitt's was too far to ride bikes and Mr. Nolan was out of town, so with Dad out of the picture we had no choice but to wait.

I always liked going over to Uncle Howard's and Aunt Mary's house. Howard was my Mom's older brother and even though their kids were off at college, we'd get a tennis ball or a stick and play fetch with their dog Duke. Another great thing about Uncle Howard was that he worked for a cookie company and whenever he stopped by our house to visit, he would pull a box of cookies out of his car trunk and give them to us. But, unfortunately if we went there for supper, Mom would tell us not to ask him for cookies, and she'd also tell us to behave. Now Uncle Howard knew Mom would always tell us not to bug him for cookies so just to wind her up, he'd slide us a box or two right when we were leaving just to see the look on Mom's face.

With the next two nights booked, all I needed to do now was just find some place to put our critters so they could make it to Saturday morning.

Chapter Six

The King of the Aquarium

M OM WOULD NOT LET us put them in the refrigerator. She had visions of crawdads climbing all over the cheese, grabbing the sliced ham, and ripping the tops off the mayonnaise or jelly jars, so there was no way we could put them in there. Unfortunately, even if they were sitting in the shade, we didn't think that they'd last very long stuck outside in the milk cartons. Therefore, we had to think of something.

I was deep in thought as I walked into the bedroom that Dad and Uncle Mack had built as an addition to our house after I was born and the family needed more space. Timmy, David and I all shared it, and our room was set up like a barracks, as Dad always told us, him being a former Marine and all. He would let us know that having our beds all in a row was like it was for him when he was at boot camp. Boot camp or not, my bed was the best place for me to do some serious thinking.

I flopped down on my bed, folded my arms behind my head and started thinking. Unfortunately no thoughts came into my head, but then just when I was about to give up, I saw it – Timmy's aquarium. Coming into the room I'd walked right past it without giving it a thought. However, seeing that aquarium gave me an idea. What better way to keep our bait alive than putting them in the aquarium, and we'd be able to watch them swim around with all the tropical fish in the tank. They'd only be there for a few days, so everything should be okay. I mean, what could possibly go wrong? Unbeknownst to me, I was quickly going to find out.

Timmy and David had gone off on their bikes somewhere so I decided that I would surprise them with my brilliant idea. I went out back, got the container with the crawdads, and brought it into our room. I opened the lid on top of the tank, and using the net from the aquarium I scooped up a couple of the crawdads and lowered the net into the tank. Once the net was in the water, they wriggled free and settled to the bottom of the tank on top of the gravel. The resident fish in the tank didn't seem too concerned, so all looked good. I scooped out the rest of the crawdads and they joined their friends on the bottom of the tank. Next came the minnows. There weren't as many of these so it was a pretty easy transfer from the milk carton to the tank for them. Again, the resident tropical fish didn't seem to mind their new neighbors much, so all continued to look good. The one exception however, was the gourami.

Now I think that the gourami had been in the tank the longest and we had dubbed him the "King of the Aquarium." The gourami was silvery in color, about an inch and a half long, and an inch high. He had two long whiskers that trailed down from his chin. He swam around the tank like he owned it and all the other fish would get out of his way when he came around. He clearly didn't like the sudden intrusion of the heathen crick dwellers into the rarefied water of his aquarium, so he immediately started in chasing the minnows. In spite of this, I figured that once they all got to know each other, they'd settle down and all would be fine.

Timmy and David got home and we all had supper. After we'd finished the dishes, I said to them, "Guys, come see what I did to save our bait."

"Whadja do now, Auggie?" Timmy asked.

"Follow me, I'll show you," I replied. At that, I led them back to our room and proud as punch I pointed to the aquarium.

"Auggie, you idiot!" Timmy screamed. "You can't do that! It'll kill all the fish!"

"Whaddya mean? How will it kill the fish? They're only going to be in there until Saturday when we go fishing," I explained.

"No, you moron, you can't mix dirty crick water with the clean water in the aquarium, that's going to cause all of my fish to die!" Timmy moaned.

I couldn't believe it, but Timmy was really getting mad – real mad.

"You are going to pay me to replace all of those fish," he snarled.

David just started laughing.

"Auggie, you've really outdone yourself on this one," he said.

"It's not funny, David!" Timmy snapped.

"Oh come on Timmy, you hardly cared about those fish anyhow," David said, still chuckling.

Then he added, "There's nothing that we can do about it now, so let's wait and see what happens. Besides, it could be kind of cool to see what the crawdads do to the fish."

The prospect of being able to witness crawdad-fish death matches in the aquarium seemed to appeal to Timmy and he calmed down a bit.

"Just think of it brother," David said to Timmy, "we get to see nature take its course firsthand in our own room and if nothing happens, we have them for fishing on Saturday."

Timmy nodded his head in agreement and we all sat on the floor in front of the tank and watched it like it was a TV show waiting for the big showdown between crawdad and fish. Nothing happened. Well nothing out of the ordinary. The fish swam around, a little more crowded now, and the crawdads lay on the bottom of the tank partially burrowed into the gravel with just their heads and claws sticking up. But that was it.

"This is boring," I said after about ten minutes.

"See Timmy, they're all getting along fine, and none of them are dying," I added.

"I agree, this is boring," David said. "I'm gonna see what else is up."

As he got up to leave, we heard Dad call out, "Boys, come here please!"

We all came into the kitchen where he was standing by the back door.

"Timmy and David, I need you two to come with me to Mr. Hoffman's to help move the furniture. Auggie, please mow the yard before it gets dark."

It only took about forty minutes to mow the yard, both front and back, as we didn't have that big of a lot, so I dragged the mower out of the garage, filled it with gas and set about cutting the grass. I'd be done before Timmy and David got back.

After I'd finished with the lawn and they'd gotten back we checked in on the aquarium a few more times that evening until bedtime, but nothing happened. No mass poisonings, no fish jumping out of the tank screaming for their lives. No crawdads chomping down on fish or squaring off in gladiatorial combat. Nothing. Just a bunch of fish swimming around. So we turned off the light and went to sleep.

The next morning, Friday, we awoke to a scene straight out of the apocalypse. Most of the tropical fish were floating belly-up on top of the water. Obviously, Timmy was right about not mixing the water. One crawdad had half a minnow in its claw and the other half was laying on the bottom of the tank near the filter intake. The other crawdads seemed to have all disappeared, but they were just under the gravel. Several of the remaining expensive tropical fish and unscathed minnows looked like they weren't going to make it through the rest of the day. However, even with all of this carnage, there was one fish who looked more angry than anything else, and that was the gourami. He was swimming around challenging anything that got near it. Even the crawdads seemed to keep their distance.

"You owe me, Auggie," Timmy said calmly, looking straight through me. "Not only are you going to pay me for all of those fish, you are going to completely clean that tank."

"Uggh," I gulped. I had no idea that this was going to be the result of my "great idea."

"Okay, okay, I'll pay you whatever I owe you for the fish," I told him.

All I had was my paper route money, which I'd been saving for a BB gun. I had no idea how much of this would be going to buy replacement fish, but all I knew was that the BB gun just got kicked further down the road.

We salvaged the rest of the minnows and crawdads from the tank, and the next day it was only Dad and me who went fishing at McDevitt's Pond. Timmy and David were meeting up with some of their school friends to play baseball and didn't want to go, and Dean was helping at his dad's construction business. The bass weren't biting, so after about an hour we turned the rest of the bait loose into what would be their third home in as many days, not counting their time in the milk cartons, and left them to fend for themselves.

When I got home, I looked in the tank, and there he was, the gourami, all one and a half inches of him swimming around looking for something to either eat or fight. I can't say for sure, but I think that he shot me a cross look from the corner of his eye as he glided by. Clearly, he was the undisputed king of the aquarium.

Chapter Seven

NELLIE

TIMMY HAD CALMED DOWN some and said that he'd help me clean out the aquarium. I think that he volunteered since he probably didn't trust me to do it right, and I for one couldn't blame him. We got a small bucket and into it went our one surviving fish, Mr. Gourami. 'King of the Aquarium' he may be, but he's still just a fish and so he had to put up with being netted and dropped into a bucket while his home got emptied and cleaned. Cleaning out the tank and washing all the gravel and stuff that goes in it took most of the afternoon. Once we were all done and all the remnants of the crick and its critters had been sanitized out of the tank, we put the gourami back in it. He swam around all regal-like, but clearly he was lonely as it was just him in there. Even the ceramic bubbling deep-sea diver standing on a chest of gold in the middle of the tank wouldn't hold his interest. Again, I honestly think that he gave me another dirty look when he swam by the front of the tank. Hey, I'll apologize to my brother for ruining his aquarium, and killing his fish, but I'm just not going to apologize to a fish! In the end, I owed Timmy $15.00 for new fish. Every two weeks, I usually netted about $25.00 from my paper route, so my 'brilliant idea' had cost me over a week's worth of delivering papers.

We all had paper routes. Timmy and David each had morning routes with about 70 customers. They delivered papers every morning except Sunday. So they always stayed up late on Saturday nights knowing that they'd be sleeping in a bit on Sunday. The Sunday morning paper was the big one with the extra big sports section and all the other sections with lots of ads. My paper route was for the Sunday morning paper and the afternoon paper, which went out every day except for Sundays. So every day, I was delivering a newspaper.

Most folks got both the morning and the afternoon papers to get their news. Since the Sunday paper was so big, there wasn't any need for a Sunday afternoon paper. I had about sixty customers on my route and it took me about an hour and a half to deliver all of my newspapers. Most Sunday mornings I did my route myself, getting up at 4:30, grabbing my newspaper bag, and heading out to deliver papers. However, if it was raining or during the winter when it was bitterly cold or snowing, then Dad would usually help me, and with him using the car, we could get done in no time. This Sunday was a beautiful summer morning, so I was on my own.

My route started about four blocks away from our house, but the delivery guy that dropped off the paper bundles for each paperboy drove right down our street. His name was Earl, and he was probably around sixty years old. He had gray hair and always wore an old baseball cap that had the logo of the local seed corn company on it. He kept it tilted back and cocked a bit to the right. He had a friendly smile and I'd always wave to him if he drove by while I was walking to my starting point or say good morning to him if I got there before he did. One time when it was raining, he offered to give me a ride if I sat in the back of his pickup so that I could chuck my bundle off at my stop. This way he didn't have to get out of his truck and grab the bundle, and I didn't have to walk to my stop. Plus, being able to ride in the open bed of the pickup and heave out my bundle was a blast. If I was in the back of his truck, Earl would do a bit of a detour hitting two drop points before mine instead of going directly to mine. I didn't mind because it only took an extra five minutes and I could chuck more bundles. After a few times, I just waited for Earl at the end of my driveway and jumped in his truck when he came by. We did the same thing for the afternoon deliveries as well.

This morning I was particularly eager to get out on my route because my Uncle Alan's dog Nellie was about to give birth to a litter of pups and I was hoping that I'd see her out in her kennel. My Uncle Alan was my mom's youngest brother, and he and his wife Joan and their kids lived four blocks away from us and were on my paper route. Their kids were a lot younger than us, so when we went over there we were more babysitters than playmates but we still had fun with them.

Uncle Alan and his older brother Howard both had English Setters, and it was Howard's dog, Duke that sired this litter so these pups were already family. Nellie had a mainly white coat with flecks of brown throughout and her face had one big patch of black fur just below and behind her right eye. Duke also had a white coat but with tons of black flecks all over him. They both had long silky fringes on the back of their legs, under their bellies and on their tails. While I liked Duke, I knew Nellie better and she was the friendliest dog.

Nellie's kennel was in their side yard and when I was delivering papers, I always stopped and pet her through the fence when I got to their house. Sometimes in the afternoon, if Nellie was out, I'd open the gate, go into the backyard, give Aunt Joan her paper, then drop my bag of papers on the porch, grab a ball or toy and play with Nellie for a few minutes. Without a doubt, Nellie was my favorite dog and so that morning I was ready and waiting when Earl pulled up to my driveway.

"G'morning, Earl," I said to him through the open truck window as he rolled to a stop.

Earl was the only grownup that I called by his first name. I never even got a chance to ask him his last name so that I could call him Mr. Last Name because when we first met, he just said, "Everyone calls me Earl, so call me Earl." My parents said that it'd be okay, since that was what he wanted, and so we all just called him Earl.

I tossed my canvas newspaper bag into the back of his pickup and then hopped in after it. I sat on the bundles of newspapers with my back to the side of the truck's bed. We headed down the street and came to the drop off point for the route next to mine. Earl slowed to a stop and I chucked the bundle of papers out to land right on the sidewalk on the corner.

"You good?" Earl shouted.

"Yep," I answered.

At that, I sat back down and got the next bundle positioned to toss out. He drove the three blocks to the next route, which was Brad Jansen's route. I knew Brad from seeing him around and from Little League, and he was always friendly. We got along well, but since he lived several blocks away, we never really hung out much. Brad was waiting for us when we pulled up and when we stopped I just handed him his bundle.

"Hi ya Auggie, hi ya Earl," Brad said as he took hold of his bundle.

"See ya Auggie, see ya Earl," He called out as we drove off.

"See ya, Brad," I said as we pulled away.

Seeing how it wasn't even five o'clock in the morning yet, this was more than enough conversation for all of us. Earl backtracked a bit to get to my drop off point, and once he stopped, I threw my bundle down and holding my canvas bag in one hand I jumped out of the truck and landed on the grass beside the street.

"See ya, Earl," I called out to him as the truck started moving away.

I didn't hear his reply, but he gave a friendly wave through his open window and drove off up the street.

I cut open my bundle of papers, put half of them into my bag, and wrapped up the other half, as I would be coming back to them once I'd delivered my first load. Thirty minutes later, I was back to my start point and I loaded the rest of the papers into the bag. Uncle Alan and Aunt Joan lived on Oakbrook Road near the end of my route, so by the time that I got to their house, the sun was already up, as was my Aunt Joan. I opened their storm door and put the paper inside, Aunt Joan saw me and said softly,

"Auggie, come on in and see Nellie, and her pups."

"Yes, please," I answered right away.

"She gave birth yesterday morning and we've been busy ever since getting her squared away," she told me.

They'd moved Nellie out of her kennel, brought her inside, and set up a bed for her in the corner of their kitchen in a large cardboard box with the front cut down so she could go in and out easily. In the bottom of the box was a heating pad covered by blankets and on the blanket lay Nellie on her side with one, two, three, four, five, six pups all squirming to nurse milk from her. She had a pained expression on her face with all those pups pushing at her, but she was putting up with it and being just the best momma dog she could be. Periodically Nellie would raise her head, stretch out her tongue and give however many pups within her reach a good lick. She was either cleaning something off their fur, or just letting them know that she loved them, but more than likely, she was doing both!

"You should take one of these pups," Uncle Alan said to me as he walked into the kitchen.

Uncle Alan was in his mid-thirties and was one of my favorite uncles because he was always doing something cool. He and Uncle Howard used their dogs for pheasant hunting and I really wanted to go hunting with them sometime, but hadn't been asked yet.

"Boy, I'd love to have one, but I don't know if my mom will let us have a dog," I said, barely containing my excitement.

"You leave her to me," Uncle Alan said with a sly smile on his face.

"Now get me my Sunday paper, and get yourself home," he cracked good-naturedly to me.

"Yessir, on my way!"

I gave Nellie a quick pat and headed out the door to finish my route. All I could think of the whole way home was training my soon-to-be dog how to hunt pheasants with my uncles.

Chapter Eight

DAD AND THE PUPPIES

IT WAS A LITTLE after six in the morning when I got home. I was too excited to try to go back to bed and besides, I'd have to be getting up anyway in about half an hour to go to Mass so I just stayed up. Dad and Mom were already awake and in the kitchen so I plunged headfirst into telling them all about Nellie and the pups.

"Dad, can we go over there after church?" I asked, barely containing myself. "Uncle Alan said that I could have one of the pups!"

"Oh, did he now," said Dad.

I thought that I detected a slight bit of annoyance in his voice, but I wasn't sure. I shot a quick pleading glance at Mom hoping that she'd come to my aid but she was busy making coffee and didn't seem to be listening to our conversation.

My brothers and I had been pestering our parents for years to get us a dog. Heck, even Polly had been doing it, so it was unanimous that we all wanted a dog. Well, at least unanimous among us kids that is. However, Dad just didn't want one. He said that we'd never take care of it; he said that he'd end up having to do everything with it if we got one, and he didn't want the hassle and expense. Mom was usually fairly quiet when the topic came up, but, this time it was her brothers who had the dogs, so I felt that we had an "in" to getting one.

"Honey, I think it'd be fun to go see those pups today, so let's do that this afternoon right after lunch," Mom said to Dad.

She set Dad's coffee down in front of him and gave his shoulder a loving squeeze as she sat down joining him at the table with her cup of coffee.

"We can go see them, but we're not getting one," Dad answered.

I started to launch into my spiel, which I'd only said at least a hundred times before, about how we'd all be good owners, and how we'd all do everything for the dog and that he'd not have to do anything, but Mom cut me off saying;

"August, go wake up Polly and your brothers, and start getting ready for Mass."

Mom and Dad were really the only ones that called me "August." I mean other than most teachers and Principal Antonucci, but that's another story. I was too slow in the head to catch the smile in Mom's voice; otherwise, I would've left the kitchen feeling hopeful. As it was, I left the kitchen trying to think of how I could convince Dad that he was wrong about getting a dog.

When my brothers and Polly heard about Nellie's pups they couldn't wait to go over there. Now it was all four of us putting the pressure on Dad, but he wouldn't budge. As soon as we got home from church, I quickly changed out of my good clothes getting back into my normal clothes and hurried into the kitchen.

"Mom, how soon can we head over to Uncle Alan and Aunt Joan's?"

She was still in her church clothes and Dad was still in his suit. They were taking far too long to get ready.

"August, relax," Dad said. "Don't worry, those puppies aren't going anywhere. Let's have some lunch then we'll head over."

While Mom and Dad went and changed, Timmy, David, Polly, and I all made sandwiches as fast as we could. We were already almost finished eating when they came back into the kitchen. We'd even made each of them a sandwich. Although I don't think Dad was too excited to be eating a peanut butter and jelly sandwich, even though its middle was stuffed with potato chips.

Peanut butter and grape jelly was too mushy, so to make the sandwich properly, you had to put a layer of potato chips in between the jelly and the peanut butter to give it that perfect bit of crunch. While I'm sure that Dad wanted to torture us a bit more by making us wait, Mom was having none of it, so she made him eat the sandwich, said, "Let's go," and hustled us all out the door. I laughed at Dad trying to get the last bites of his PB&J as Mom shooed him up and out of the kitchen.

Since their house was only a few blocks away, we started walking over. Well Mom and Dad walked, Polly, my brothers and me all tore out of there at full speed and left our parents in the dust.

When we got to my uncle's house, we went straight into the kitchen to see the pups. They were all snuggled up against their mom sound asleep. They were way too young to handle and play with so all we could really do was stare at them and ooh and aww. Fortunately, my Uncle Howard and Aunt Mary showed up and they brought their dog Duke with them. Duke just kind of nosed around the pups and didn't show any real interest, so Uncle Howard said:

"Why don't you kids take Duke outside and throw his ball for him."

We didn't need to be told twice, so we grabbed his ball and ran outside to play fetch with Duke leaving Mom, Dad, my aunts and my uncles all sitting chatting and laughing in Alan and Joan's living room.

"I wonder if they're in there trying to talk Mom and Dad into letting us get a puppy." Timmy pondered aloud.

"I sure hope so!"

"Auggie, you really have your heart set on a dog, don't you?" Polly asked.

"Absolutely, don't you Polly?"

"Yeah, it'll be fun, especially if you do all the work!"

"I won't mind. If we get a pup, I can't wait to train it to hunt just like Nellie and Duke! Besides, Dad'll help me if we get one."

"Dad doesn't bird hunt anymore Auggie, he's always working or doing other stuff." Timmy said.

"Well, hopefully he'll let me..."

I didn't really finish what I was saying, I just left the words hanging in the air as my mind wandered to thoughts of working a dog through the fence lines and hedgerows on the edges of cornfields looking for pheasants.

Being outside we couldn't hear what the grownups were talking about, but for the most part, it looked like Uncles Alan and Howard together with Mom on one side, talking at Dad on the other. Aunt Joan and Aunt Mary had gone off to the kitchen. When we came in, Dad called all four of us together, and with everyone else looking on, Dad told us we could pick out the puppy that we wanted. He went on to tell us that we had to exercise it every day, we had to pick up after it, had to do this and had to do that, and lots of other stuff. But honestly, not a one of us heard a single word after he'd said that we could get one of the pups! The one thing I did hear was my Uncle Alan saying that we'd have to wait eight more weeks before we could take one home. However, he also said we could come over whenever we wanted to visit them.

In the end, we picked a male whose right eye peeked out from a big black splotch on the right side of his face and who had brownish colored "eyebrows" above each eye. His coat was white with black flecking throughout his body. It looked like he'd run up a chimney pipe wearing a fur coat! After a lot of arguing, we landed on the name Jake for our dog. Timmy was the one who suggested that name.

"Dad, can we train Jake for hunting?" I asked.

"We'll see, my boy. But if you really want to take Jake hunting, then I'll leave his training up to you, and depending on how you do with it, maybe, just maybe, we'll do some bird hunting next year."

"Don't worry Auggie, I'll be around to help you and your dad train ol' Jake here," Uncle Alan said with a wink and a smile.

Later that night right at bedtime, Dad was tucking us in, and I had to ask him, "Hey Dad, what made you change your mind?"

"Well Auggie," sometimes he called me Auggie, especially when he was relaxed, "It's like this. Your mom gave me that look, and when I took a deep breath and started to answer her to tell her how it wasn't a good idea, that our house was too busy, and all my other reasons why the answer had to be no, I looked up and my eyes landed on both of her brothers standing behind her and they were both grinning and shaking their heads at me knowing full well that I didn't stand a chance. So I did the most honorable thing possible, and retreated quietly and humbly to a yes. And that, my boy is why you've got a dog."

Chapter Nine

SUMMER VACATION

SUMMER WAS SLIPPING AWAY as August, the month, was just around the corner. Once August hit, then it was only a matter of time before we'd be back in school, with no more lazy days spent sitting in the backyard trying to figure out what to do. But before that happened, we had our favorite week of the summer coming up and that was our family vacation to Big Spirit Lake which is in the northwestern corner of the state right on the Minnesota line. It was a four-hour drive to the small lake house that we'd rented. It was one of several that formed a small "resort" on the lake. As far as resorts go, it would best be described as "rustic."

The whole place was owned by Mr. and Mrs. Miller, a real nice older couple who reminded everyone of their grandparents. It was a group of about fifteen to twenty small two or three bedroom lake houses, or cabins as we called them, clustered in a semicircle facing the lake and within walking distance to the beach. Behind them was the office building, which doubled as a general store. The store was small, but good enough for what you needed at the lake. You could buy groceries, kitchen stuff, candy, and other necessities. But most of all, it had the funkiest coolest soda pop vending machine located outside on the porch next to the door.

There were several large maple and oak trees scattered around the property, so each cabin had ample shade to keep it cool from the midday sun. None of them had air conditioning, everyone just kept their doors and windows wide open relying on the window screens and screen doors to keep the bugs out. When all the units were rented out, there was always a constant cacophony of slamming screen doors as kids ran in and out letting the doors bang shut behind them. Of course, this was always followed by a chorus of parents yelling at them to quit slamming the door! All of us kids in every unit were guilty of ignoring this admonition, as it wouldn't be a summer at the lake without slamming screen doors and running kids.

I couldn't wait to get there. We'd all pitched in and packed the night before, loading the car as best we could. We stuffed everything into the back of our station wagon, leaving nary an inch to spare as we were loaded to the gills. As always, Dad insisted that we were going to leave the next morning at eight o'clock sharp and as always, we'd be lucky to get out of there by nine. This year was no exception. On Saturday morning, my alarm clock went off at seven, and I sprang out of bed throwing on my jeans and T-shirt as I headed barefoot out to the kitchen.

Timmy and David had stayed up after getting home from their morning paper routes so they were eating breakfast when I turned the corner into the kitchen.

"I call the window seat behind Mom," I announced when I sat down.

"You can't call your seat until we're all outside, Auggie," my brother Timmy said with a slight annoyance to his voice.

Uggh, he was right. In all my excitement, I'd forgotten the rules of 'shotgun.' You can't call shotgun or your preferred seat in the car until all of the passengers were outside, and in view of the car. I didn't make these rules up, these rules were universally understood and practiced everywhere that there were cars, or so I was told.

"Besides it doesn't matter since we rotate every hour," David said.

He was right, but I always thought that the first hour was the longest, and so I wanted to try to get the best seat in the car. As it was, Dad always drove, and Mom always sat in the front passenger seat, the shotgun seat, which is why we never yelled "shotgun" when all of us were going somewhere because Mom was always shotgun by default. That left the three spots across the back seat and the dreaded middle spot between Mom and Dad on the front seat. Three up front, and three in back, perfect for a family of six. Perfect that is unless you're the kid stuck between his parents for an hour in the front middle.

The best spots were the window seats behind Mom and Dad and the worst spots were the middle seats with the absolute worst being the front middle. On our first trip to Spirit Lake a few years ago, my parents instituted the stop-every-hour-and-rotate rule to make it fair. A four hour drive, four kids, four spots to sit in the car, it was a match made in heaven. The great thing was that whoever was stuck in the front middle would ask how many minutes had gone by at least twenty times during the one hour up front!

Seating order arranged and me stuck up front for the first hour, we set off promptly sometime before nine o'clock, but clearly well past eight. Stopping every hour, we got there a little before two in the afternoon. We pulled up to the parking space behind the office, and Dad went in to get the key. All of us kids piled out of the car and headed towards the lake.

It was a hot sunny day with a slight breeze gently rustling the leaves on the trees. At the shoreline, we looked for rocks to skip. Since it was the end of July, most of the good skipping rocks had already been skipped into the lake, but if you looked hard enough you could find some. Also, right out front, by where we were looking for skipping rocks, the property had a dock with several motorboats tied up that were available for rent. These boats were aluminum rowboats and each one had a small outboard motor clamped to the stern. They were great for putt-putting around on the lake for fishing. Our resort didn't have any of those big speedboats for waterskiing and such; they only had these small boats. But we didn't care, because this was the only time we ever got to go in a boat, so for us they were perfectly fine. However, if we took one out, no more than four of us could fit into it, which meant that we had to take turns if everyone wanted to go. Dad would sit in the back and run the motor driving the boat, two of us would sit on the middle bench, and one of us would sit up front on the bow bench. Since each of us wanted to sit in the bow, Dad would make us rotate seats to keep us from fighting over it. Rotating seating arrangements were big in the Thumb family!

Spirit Lake was a big lake for Iowa and had great fishing, especially for bass, crappie and perch. Sometimes you could catch walleye or even a muskie, but getting a muskie was a pretty rare event. In all our trips to the lake, we'd never caught one. We usually went out fishing in the morning or in the evening right after dinner.

"Kids get up here!" Mom called to us. "Help unpack the car, and that way we can all go down to the lake," she added.

Now that made perfect sense, but that wasn't what we all wanted to do. We wanted to explore the area and go swimming. However, it wasn't fair to leave the unpacking to Mom, so we all ran up and helped unload.

Once Dad had unlocked the cabin and opened the door, we all ran in to claim our preferred sleeping spots.

"I get the top bunk in here," David shouted.

He'd been just a hair quicker than Timmy in getting into the room, so Timmy was stuck with the bottom bunk in that room.

"I get the top bunk in here!" I said as I went into the other bedroom.

"Not a chance, Squirt," Polly said to me with her authoritative older sister voice.

"If I have to put up with you sleeping in this room with me, then I absolutely get the top bunk."

Polly had taken to calling me Squirt as well, and I really didn't like it, but when she did it, I didn't seem to mind as much as when one of my brothers called me it, so again, I begrudgingly accepted it.

Once we all unpacked and moved in, we set out to explore the campgrounds and see what was up before we went swimming. Right in the middle of the big grassy area that was in front of the cabins was the trampoline. It was a big rectangular trampoline and it was open to anyone who dared to use it. When parents were around it was pretty well-mannered usage, but the moment that the parents walked away it turned into a free-for-all, and at that moment, no one was using it.

"Hey guys, let's go on the trampoline!" I shouted as I ran up to it, kicked my shoes off, climbed up, and started jumping.

Last year I'd learned how to do a front flip on it and I wanted to see if I could still do one. If we were doing flips and stuff, only one person could be jumping at a time, if we were just messing around on it, there really wasn't a limit. Since there weren't any safety nets around it there was a big sign that said, "JUMP AT YOUR OWN RISK." There was also a lot of small print under the sign, but no one read it, and frankly, most of us didn't even see the sign at all.

Polly, Timmy and David sat on the edges of the tramp to hopefully catch me and keep me from hitting the ground if I went too far out of kilter on my flip attempts, and they usually did a pretty good job of that, but only if they were paying attention that is. I did a couple of flips, landed safely, and then it was Polly's turn. She's much better at the flips and jumping stuff than us boys, so we didn't need to be as careful with her. While she was jumping, three kids came walking up. It was the Samuelson's. They always came to the lake the same week that we did and over the years, we'd gotten to know them. They were from Minnesota, so we thought it was pretty cool to talk to people from another state. For the most part, they were nice and we got along well with them.

The oldest boy Andy was Polly's age but with her being a girl and all, he'd usually hang around with us. Andy was a big kid and a real good football player for his high school. The next one was Scott, and he was twelve, right between my brothers and me in age. He was okay, but sometimes he could be a bit ornery and if he ever got out of line Andy would usually rope him in. The youngest was Katie, and she was just a month younger than me. She always tried to hang around me, and I hated getting stuck with her. However, most times Polly would take her and they'd go off and do girl stuff together and us boys would play football in the lake with Andy throwing spirals to us.

"Hey guys, what's up?" Andy called out as they came up to the trampoline.

Polly had just done a flip and landed it perfectly.

"Nice flip Polly," Andy said, complimenting her.

There was something about the way Andy had said that and there was something about the way Polly reacted that caused me to pause a bit. But I just shrugged it off and didn't pay it any more mind.

"Hey Andy, hey Scott, hey Katie," we all said.

"Hey Andy, did you bring your football with ya this year?" I asked eagerly.

"I'm on your team when we play," I added.

"Yeah Auggie, I've got it somewhere," he answered.

The "somewhere" was right there in his right hand! He seemed completely distracted and I couldn't figure out why.

"Hey, Polly, let's see that flip again, you looked great doing that last one," Andy said.

"Hey Andy, you've got your ball with you, throw me a pass, I'm open!" I called out to him as I ran out on a route.

"Auggie, don't be such a dope," David said to me.

Andy tossed the ball to his brother Scott and said, "You guys go ahead and get a game going, and I'll be right over."

I couldn't figure out why Andy wanted to hang out at the trampoline instead of play football with us and then Timmy smacked me on the shoulder.

"Owww! Whad ja do that for!"

"That's for being an idiot. Can't you see that Andy likes Polly, and wants to hang out with her instead of us right now?" He asked me slightly annoyed.

"Huh, what?"

"Oh, ohhh," I said, not completely sure what he meant, but thinking that I was.

"Why can't he do that later, when we're doing something else," I half whined to whoever would listen to me.

But, with no one listening to me, we all trotted off to the beach with Katie tagging along and split up into two teams for a game of football on the beach.

"Auggie, I'll be on your team," Katie said to me.

"Sure, whatever," I replied to her, hoping that no one had heard her.

"David and me against you three," Scott quickly said before anyone could decide differently.

"Hey Auggie, you'd better watch it, I think Katie's got a crush on you," Scott said teasing me.

"I do NOT!" Katie shouted.

Katie was making it clear that she had no interest in me at all, which essentially meant that her brother had touched a nerve, and more than likely, she probably did have a crush on me.

Ugghh, I didn't need no girl having a crush on me and ruining my vacation. I just wanted to play football, swim, jump on the trampoline, fish, eat junk food, drink soda pop, and hang out for a week without any real chores to do. Now that was all going to be ruined. First, with Andy acting all goofy around Polly, and now with his little sister tagging along with me like a shadow wherever I went. Why couldn't things just stay the same as they'd always been?

Chapter Ten

Target Practice

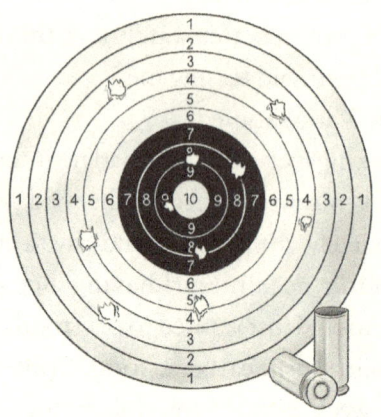

The highlight of our week was when Dad took us all to the local shooting range. It was just a couple of miles from the lake, and it was run by an old Marine named Gus Meyer that Dad knew from way back when they were both in the Marine Corps. One part of the range was set up for kids and beginners and used single shot bolt-action .22 caliber rifles with paper targets set up 25 yards out from the firing line. The targets were attached by clothespins to two wires that ran across the back of the range. The lower wire was for the bottom of the targets, and the upper one for the top of the targets. When Gus told you to do so, you went downrange, and using four wooden clothespins, clamped your target to the wires one pin at each corner.

If you shot a clothespin, Gus charged you twenty-five cents, so you wanted to make sure you didn't ever hit one. Usually all four of us kids and the Samuelson boys would go with Dad to the range while Mom stayed back to read her book by the lake. However, this time Polly said that she didn't want to go, and oddly enough, Andy didn't go either. So it was only Scott who came with us, as he'd never pass up an opportunity to go shooting.

When we got to the range, Gus greeted Dad with some Marine joke and they chatted for a bit before Gus said, "Okay boys, we're going to go over the rules before anyone goes out to the range. You will all be shooting from the prone position and no one touches a rifle until I tell you to."

He explained all of the rules to us and reminded us that if we accidentally hit a clothespin it would cost us twenty-five cents. He also told us that whoever had the best target score would win an ice cream bar from his freezer. The competition was on!

Gus took us out to the firing line and we all laid down on the ground next to a rifle. Timmy was on the end, then David, then Scott and then me. Dad stood with Gus to help supervise.

"Alright boys, keeping your muzzle pointed downrange, pick up your rifle and shoulder it," Gus commanded.

At that, we all aimed our rifles at our targets and snugged the butts up against our shoulders.

After he'd made sure that we were all in the correct position Gus said, "Pick up one round from the tray in front of you, load it into the action, and once you have the round chambered, push the bolt forward and secure it."

I sighted in my rifle on the bullseye of the target and waited for the next command.

"Boys, you are all locked and loaded, so line up your targets, and when you are ready, release your safeties and fire at will. As soon as you have shot your rifle, put your safety on, open the action by pulling the bolt all the way back, and while keeping the muzzle pointed downrange, lay the rifle down."

With Gus having exhausted all of his commands, it was time to shoot. I took my time, relaxed my breathing and flicked my safety off. Laying there on my stomach with my feet properly spread out behind me, with my left arm bent at the elbow out in front of me supporting the barrel of my rifle, and my right arm also bent at the elbow, I used my right hand to grip the stock just behind the trigger guard. Lying flat out in this position I was stable, steady, and ready to fire.

I slowly placed my right index finger on the trigger, took a deep breath, let it out slowly, and with the bullseye of the target perfectly lined up with my sights, and slowly letting my breath out, I gently squeezed the trigger. With a loud crack, my bullet went screaming towards the target. I couldn't tell for sure where it hit, but I think that I'd gotten it in the black ring around the red bullseye. If so, that'd be nine points, as the bullseye was ten. We had all shot at essentially the same time so it sounded like one big bang with all four guns going off.

We each had ten shots per target, so we repeated the above sequence for each shot and I was feeling good about my shooting. It was hard to see the little holes in the target from twenty-five yards away, but from what I could see, I thought all of mine were on the paper and most of them near the center.

"You boys are doing some mighty fine shooting," Dad said.

We were on our eighth shot when it happened. Every time that we shot, we all seemed to shoot at essentially the exact same time so it was hard to tell who shot when. This time was no different. Just as I shot so did the others, BWANGG! A loud twanging sound split the air, and to my horror, all the targets suddenly just flopped over onto the ground while bits of broken clothespin flew up into the air only to land directly underneath my target.

"Hey what was that?" Dad exclaimed.

"Boys, set your rifles down now!" Gus firmly commanded.

Gus would never call it a gun, it was a rifle. He'd taught us that. However, most of the time we called them guns. We weren't in the Marine Corps yet. Once we all had our guns set on the ground he ordered us to stand up and move back from the firing line. Only after that did he go downrange to see what had happened. He bent down and picked up the upper wire to which all of the targets were attached by their two top clothespins, well, all but one target that is.

"August Thumb," he called out with an annoyed look on his face.

"It looks like you owe me twenty-five cents! Not only did you shoot your clothespin, but your shot broke my wire!"

He was not happy.

Gus was holding up both halves of the wire and Timmy and David's targets were fine as was Scott's. Mine however was missing an upper clothespin and that was right where the wire was broken.

"Haven't ever had that happen before," Gus remarked shaking his head.

"That's a one-in-a-million shot, but now we're done for the day until I can fix this," he added.

Timmy and David looked at me and said, "Way to go, Squirt, now we can't shoot anymore."

"There's no way I hit that wire and clothespin," I argued.

"My shot was perfectly lined up on the bullseye!"

"Well, clearly you did, since it was your clothespin that was broken," Scott said quickly piling on.

"August, come here," Dad said sternly.

"You need to apologize to Mr. Meyer and you're going to owe him more than twenty-five cents to replace the wire and clothespin!"

"Dad, I swear I didn't shoot it," I moaned to no avail.

"Gus, just let me know how much it costs and I'll reimburse you for the time and materials to fix it," Dad said. "And you can trust me, it'll be coming out of Auggie's hide," he added for good measure.

What should've been a fun morning had turned into a disaster, and now everyone was sore at me. I shuffled off to the car with the guys chiding me for breaking the wire. All thoughts of winning the shooting competition and getting the ice cream bar from Gus' freezer had faded into oblivion. None of us even talked about the competition, all we could talk about was the broken wire, my errant shot, and how horrible it was that I'd ruined our trip to the range.

Dad walked into the office with Gus to settle the bill and say goodbye. David, Scott and I were at the car waiting for him and I didn't know where Timmy was. Dad came out of the office, noticed that Timmy wasn't at the car and called out for him. Just as he finished calling, Timmy came running up from the range area.

"Let's go boys," Dad said as he opened the driver's door.

Looking me square in the eyes and with a matter of fact voice Dad said, "Auggie, you owe me twelve dollars and twenty-five cents. Gus told me that it would be twelve bucks to hang a new wire for the range, and I threw in the twenty-five cents for the clothespin." Dad added.

He chuckled to himself as he said this, seeming to get a special enjoyment out of pointing out the enormity of my debt. I sighed. The good thing was that Dad wasn't one to hold a grudge or keep dredging up a past mistake, so in his mind, this was over and done with. While I really appreciated this about my dad, I just knew there was no way I could've shot that clothespin, and I wanted to tell him that. However, I also knew that if I brought it up again he'd just point out that it was my clothespin and my target, so the facts didn't support my case. Therefore, I just let it go and didn't say anything.

Unfortunately, this was turning into an expensive summer, and it was still only July!

The car ride back to the lake house was quiet as none of us really felt like talking, but as we pulled into our parking spot,

Dad asked if anyone wanted to go out on the motorboat that he'd rented for the week.

"I'll go," said Timmy.

"Me too," added David.

"My folks told me to come right home after shooting, so I can't go," said Scott. "Thanks for taking me shooting with you Mr. Thumb," he added all pleasant and polite like.

It was sickening how fake Scott could be. The way he said it to my dad just ticked me off. I guess it was because at that point, I was everyone's enemy, but I don't know, there was just something about how he said it, that even if I hadn't ruined our trip it still probably would've bothered me.

"What about you, Auggie, do you want to go out on the boat?" Dad asked.

"No, I don't wanna do nuthin' now," I mumbled.

"Suit yourself then. Timmy and David get your stuff and if Polly's around see if she wants to go as well."

Timmy, David, Polly and Dad went out in the motorboat and I went and sulked on my bunk bed, annoyed as all get out at the whole world right then.

Chapter Eleven

"On the House"

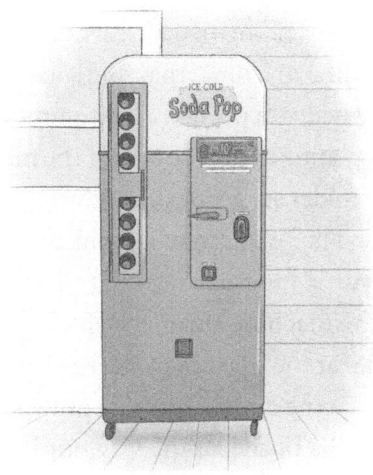

It was midafternoon when they got back. Mom was sitting on the dock reading her book and soaking up the sun. Me on the other hand hadn't moved out of my room, since I wasn't done feeling sorry for myself. Try as I might I just couldn't let it go, I kept turning it over and over in my mind. No matter how I looked at it, I couldn't for the life of me picture myself shooting that clothespin.

"Hey Auggie, we're going to the trampoline," Timmy shouted up towards the cabin.

"Okay, I'll come down later," I answered half-heartedly.

I decided that I couldn't hide inside all day, and besides, no one was paying me any attention, so while I still had a dime to my name, I decided to head over to the Miller's store behind the cabins and get a bottle of soda pop from the vending machine. This vending machine was the coolest one ever. Most of the vending machines that sold soda pop were stocked with cans and when you pushed a button the can would drop down into an opening at the bottom of the machine. This one however was an older style stocked with eight individual rows of glass bottles. The rows ran at a slight downhill angle from right to left, with a long narrow clear glass door on the left hand side of the machine through which you could see the soda pop bottles at the bottom of the rows.

You could open the door before you put your money in, but you couldn't pull a bottle all the way out because two metal rods ran from top to bottom on each side of the bottles so that only the neck of the bottles stuck out. Once you put your money into the machine and turned the lever, the rods flipped out, enabling you to pull out one bottle. Then the bottle next up in the row rolled down into place and the rods closed. The machine had everything from orange soda to grape soda, to colas, and most of all it had my favorite – root beer.

As I got there, I saw Scott Samuelson standing in front of the vending machine with his leg propping the door open. I couldn't tell what he was doing until I got closer. But then I saw. He had pulled a bottle as far forward as he could until the rods blocked it. The bottle was out just far enough to get a cup under it and once he had it in that position, he'd pried off its top with a bottle opener and was filling his cup with the soda pop that was pouring out!

"Hey, whaddya doing!" I yelled at him. "That's stealing!"

Scott looked up, saw me and took off running just as I got to the vending machine. He'd opened up two bottles, which both lay in their slots dribbling soda pop all down the front of the machine making a big puddle on the porch. I couldn't believe it! He'd run off leaving the half-empty bottles oozing soda pop in the machine. As I stood there surveying the damage Mr. Miller came out.

"Auggie Thumb, what have you done?" He exclaimed. "You're stealing my soda pop and making a mess!"

"Honest, Mr. Miller, it wasn't me!"

"Well there ain't nobody else standing here now is there? And you're holding the door open! Caught you red-handed I did! Just wait till your parents hear about this!"

I couldn't take it. Not this time. No way! This wasn't happening. I didn't say a word, I just spun around and lit outta there in the same direction as that no-account Scott Samuelson had gone.

"Git back here boy!" Mr. Miller yelled out. "Runnin' ain't gonna do you no good, I'm just gonna tell your parents when they stop by!"

In two steps, I was off the porch following after Scott who'd run off behind the store towards the road out away from the lake. When I caught up to him Scott was just standing there leaning against a fence post with the stupidest grin on his face laughing at me.

"Hey sucker," he sneered at me.

"You just ain't havin' the best day, now are ya?"

That was more than I could stand. I came right up to him and said, "Scott, you're going right back there and tell Mr. Miller that it was you who opened those bottles and not me!"

"Fat chance of that happening, I'm outta here!" He replied.

As soon as he said that, he pushed away from the fence post and started to walk away. Now Scott might've been a year older than me, but he wasn't that much bigger than me. Besides I'd grown up wrestling with not just two older and bigger brothers but also with my dad, who started wrestling with us before we could even crawl. In Iowa, if you didn't know anything else, you knew how to wrestle. So, I simply crouched down and shot in under his arms driving my right shoulder into his belly just above his waist and as soon as my shoulder hit his gut, using both arms, I grabbed him around his thighs and scooped his legs up in a perfect double-leg takedown.

As we were going down, I said, "Not on my watch!"

Flailing in the air, Scott's cup flew out of his hand, spilling cola everywhere. He tried to twist out of it, but with his legs wrapped up in my arms, he had no choice but to use his hands to keep his face from hitting the gravel as he fell. I drove him into the ground with my shoulder and immediately spun on top of his back, using my body weight to pin him down. He let out a big uummphh sound when he hit the ground and after the initial shock wore off he was mad.

He snorted, snarled, and made a weak attempt to twist onto his right side trying to hit me with his left elbow. However, I was expecting something like that and simply turned my face out of the way, and his elbow went harmlessly nowhere. Laying on top of him I pushed him down, flattening him into the gravel. In spite of me having complete control of him, he kept pumping his arms and kicking his legs trying to get out from under me, but clearly, he didn't know anything about wrestling. While all of this was going on, he kept hollering about how he was going to beat me into a pulp and a whole bunch of other things that I can't repeat.

Ignoring what he was saying, and pressing down on his back, I slid my left arm under his left armpit, up over his neck, and cupped the back of his neck in my left hand, getting him into a perfect Half Nelson. I then slid my right arm under his right arm and grabbed the top of his right wrist with my hand. I pulled his wrist down and back, bending his right arm at the elbow so that I could hold his arm in a twisted position against his back in what we called the "Chicken Wing." I now had complete control of Scott. I worked him up to a sitting position and then by keeping pressure on the back of his neck, forcing his left arm high in the air, and controlling his right arm, I pulled him up to his feet.

"Let go of me!" He screeched. "Let go of me right now! My brother's gonna kill you when he finds out!"

Once again, I just ignored him. The thought of a twelve-year-old needing a sixteen year old to beat up an eleven-year-old was just too ridiculous to even consider.

"Scotty, we're heading back to Mr. Miller's store and you're gonna tell him the truth."

I must admit that I did take some joy in calling him Scotty instead of Scott.

"The heck I am! I'm gonna get you in trouble for breaking my arm!"

"It ain't broken yet!" I replied. "However, if you don't get going, I may just break it, and then you can go ahead and get me in trouble!"

Keeping him in front of me, we marched towards the front of the Miller's store. Whenever Scott tried to resist I just pushed his right arm a little bit higher up his back until he stopped.

We stepped up on the porch and I called out to Mr. Miller.

"Mr. Miller, can you come out here, please!"

"Hey, what's going on here?" He exclaimed as he swung open the store's screen door and stepped out on the porch. "Auggie, what in tarnation are you doing to him? Let him go now!"

"Not until he tells you what he did," I said.

"I didn't do nuthin," Scott stammered choking back tears.

Man, he could really turn on the emotions when it suited him. But, I wasn't falling for it, and I sure didn't want Mr. Miller falling for it either. I pushed Scott's right arm up just a bit higher and said,

"Tell him what you did!"

Unfortunately, Scott was smarter than I'd given him credit for and all he did was just cry out that I was hurting him, so Mr. Miller, feeling sorry for him, put his hand on Scott's right shoulder and told me to release him right then and there. I had no choice, so I let go of his neck and slid my left arm out from under his arm. But before I let go of his right arm I suddenly remembered the bottle opener. He had to have it in one of his pockets.

"Mr. Miller," I quickly said. "I didn't steal from you, but if you make Scott empty his pockets, I'm sure you'll find a bottle opener in one of them, and if he denies that it's his, I'll bet his mom would identify it."

At that, I released my grip on Scott's right wrist and as the words that I'd just said sunk into his thick skull he turned beet red and Mr. Miller's grip suddenly tightened on Scott's shoulder.

"Well, Mr. Samuelson, let's see what's in your pockets."

Whenever grownups call you by your last name and use Mister, you know the gig's up and you're in for it, and it was no different now. Arguing with me was one thing, but arguing with Mr. Miller was a whole nuther thing, and Scott wasn't up for that. Having no other choice and probably wishing he were miles away, Scott put his hand in his pocket and pulled out the bottle opener.

"I'll take that," Mr. Miller said to Scott. "And just tell your folks that they can stop by the store to pick it up anytime they'd like."

Scott handed him the bottle opener and as he turned to leave, with his face all red and puffy he looked right at me and through gritted teeth he said, "This ain't over Thumb, not by a long shot," and sputtering mad and full of shame he ran off towards his family's cabin.

As much as I wanted to snap an answer back at him, I let it go unanswered. Honestly, the adrenalin was still pumping through my veins and I was on cloud nine. I had wrestled him to the ground, controlled him with ease, and most of all had proven my innocence to Mr. Miller.

"Mr. Miller, I'm sorry for running off like that, but I had to get him before he got away and I wanted to make sure that you knew the truth."

"I will admit that seeing you take off like a scalded cat shocked me some, but when you came back with the Samuelson kid all tied up in knots, it took everything I had not to laugh out loud. Now, you go on home, that's enough excitement for one day."

"Yessir."

"But Auggie, before you go, didn't you want a root beer? And don't worry, it's on the house!"

Sipping an ice cold Frostie Root Beer that was "on the house" while walking back to the cabin made me feel all grown up. Actually, that was the first time an adult had ever given me something that was "on the house."

"On the house," yeah, I liked that...

I finished my root beer on my walk back to our cabin taking my last sip just before I got to the door. Even though I still had that twelve dollar and twenty-five cent bill to pay for the broken wire, I felt on top of the world. I just couldn't stop thinking about how I'd taken Scott Samuelson down, dragged him back to the store and proven to Mr. Miller that I was innocent. How I wasn't even scared to do it, and how I didn't even hesitate. That was such a good feeling. "Good" was the best word to describe how I felt. Good, because I'd done the right thing. Good, because I wasn't mean to Scott. Good, because I exposed the truth to Mr. Miller. It doesn't always have to be great, or awesome, or fantastic. Sometimes, good is all it needs to be, and this was one of those times.

Chapter Twelve

Brotherly Love

I DECIDED NOT TO tell my parents about what had happened between Scott and me, well at least not until I could tell David and Timmy. As soon as I walked in the door, Timmy came up to me and said,

"Auggie, I've got something to show you."

"Okay and I've got something to tell you," I replied.

"C'mere and look at this, Squirt." Timmy motioned me to follow him into his bedroom, and there laid out on his bunk were all four targets which he'd taken from the range.

"I put these in the order in which I pulled them from the wire."

"I didn't know you'd taken those," I exclaimed.

"Yeah, I went and got them when Dad went in to talk to Gus and you guys all headed for the car. So here's mine, then David's, then Scott's, and here's yours. Unfortunately, we didn't sign them before we clipped them to the wire, so there's no way to prove whose is whose, but as I said, these are in the order that I pulled them down."

Looking at the targets, I counted eight holes in both Timmy and David's targets, only six holes in Scott's, and more importantly, ten holes in mine!

On mine, two of the ten holes were in the upper right corner, where the blown up clothespin had been. One of the holes was exactly where the clothespin would've been holding the target and the other was right near it. There's no way that I could have ten bullet holes in my target unless someone else had also been shooting at it, since none of us had taken more than eight shots!

"This proves Scott shot my clothespin! What a dink! I can't wait to show Dad!" I shouted.

"Hang on a minute, Auggie, all it proves is that one target has six holes. If you accuse Scott, he'll probably just claim that his target was one of the ones that had eight holes in it and that you just poked two additional holes in your target to pin the blame on him. Without our names on the targets, or without

Gus or Dad having seen which target was in which spot before I took them down, we can't prove it was Scott that shot your clothespin and caused the wire to break. We've gotta get him to confess, and I think that I know just the person to help us make that happen."

"Who's that? Whaddya gonna do?"

"Patience little brother, patience. Let me get this figured out, just sit tight."

At that moment, David came into the room to tell us that supper was ready. With both of them in the room, I recounted everything that had happened at Miller's store that afternoon, especially how I'd wrestled Scott to the ground and gotten him in a Half Nelson.

"Good for you, well done Squirt," David said.

Even when they were being nice they couldn't resist calling me Squirt now.

He gave me a light-hearted smack on the shoulder and said, "What a tough guy!"

He said that with a smile on his face and then added, "But don't go getting all full of yourself, cuz next time it might turn out differently, but regardless, I'm proud of you for sticking up for yourself and not letting him get away with stealing from Mr. Miller."

After Timmy showed David the targets and explained what he thought had happened at the range, David was ticked off.

"We should get him for this," David said. "It ain't right for him to get away with this and leave Auggie stuck paying the bill."

"If what I think will work, works, then I'm pretty sure that we'll get a confession out of him," Timmy said.

Our conversation came to an abrupt end as Mom called us to supper and we all headed outside to the picnic table for burgers and hotdogs.

After supper, it was David's and my turn to clean up and I saw Timmy talking to Polly. I had no idea what he said to her, but I could see that she was really listening to him.

Mom and Dad went down to the lake and walked out on the dock. We all ran over to the trampoline to see who was out there. A lot of times in the evenings, after supper the kids would gather at the trampoline and get games of Kick-the-Can, football, or Frisbee going, or just mess around on the trampoline trying to double-jump each other. Tonight there were just a few little kids and their parents at the trampoline, so double jumping each other was out of the question. If you're not familiar with double jumping, what you do is time your jump to land right next to and right after the other person to steal their bounce. Or, if you land right before them you can get all their energy and go sky high. It's a lot of fun, but not really all that safe, and not the best thing to do with little kids, since a big kid can launch little kids clear off the trampoline and into the dirt which just doesn't go over well with their parents.

Since the trampoline was out for the moment, we were standing around trying to think of what to do when I noticed Andy and Katie Samuelson walking up. Andy had his football with him, and as they came up to us, Andy told me to go out for a pass. Dutifully I sprinted towards the lake, cut to my left, and he lofted a perfect spiral to me that I caught with both hands!

"Andy, great throw! Let's get a game going!" I shouted.

Before he could answer, I was surprised to hear Polly say, "Yes, let's get a game going! Auggie, you, Timmy and David against Andy, Katie, and me."

Uggh, I didn't want to be on a team with my brothers, I wanted to be on Andy's team, but at least Katie wasn't on my team. It was us against Andy and the two girls, so we should be able to take them, which was fair enough, I guess.

David was our quarterback, I hiked the ball and then Timmy and I both ran out as receivers. Katie tried to cover me and Polly was on Timmy. The rusher had to count to three Mississippi before he could rush the passer so Andy was standing there counting one Mississippi, two Mississippi, and when he hit three Mississippi, he ran towards David. David didn't waste any time holding the ball, he just heaved it in the general direction of both me and Timmy. Timmy caught it, turned, and ran into the end zone. One pass, one catch and one touchdown. This was going to be too easy!

For kick-offs we punted the ball, and since he'd scored, Timmy did the honors. Andy caught it but I couldn't believe what happened next. Instead of running it back for a certain touchdown, he pitched it to Polly to let her run it back. We were playing two-hand touch so it was an easy touch to stop Polly after she went about two steps. Katie ran up with her arms folded in front of her, and 'blocked' me by bumping into me.

"The play's over, Katie! No need to run into me, ya goof."

"Auggie, have some manners will ya," David said to me. "You don't have to be a moron all the time, ya know."

Here I am trying to play football and suddenly I'm getting a lecture on manners from a brother who had trouble even spelling the word manners.

We played a few more series of downs, each of us taking turns, but I noticed that everyone was kinda losing interest in the game. Mainly because Polly and Andy were taking too much time talking and looking at each other instead of playing. After a bit, Katie said she was bored and she wandered off towards their cabin.

The next thing I knew I saw Polly and Andy holding hands. What the heck was up with that? I could tell that Polly was saying something important to Andy cuz the look on his face got all serious-like and then he said something to Polly, turned, and quickly headed back to his cabin.

Timmy, David and I headed back to our cabin to get our swimsuits to go in the lake and Polly walked out on the dock to talk with Mom and Dad. After we'd changed, we headed back to the beach. We were going to jump off the dock right where Polly, Mom and Dad were sitting and try to soak them with some well-aimed cannonballs. However, just as we got to the dock, Andy came walking up, and gosh darn it, he actually looked to be dragging his little brother with him. Yep, sure enough, he had a real firm grip on Scott's arm and Scott didn't look none too happy about it.

"Hold up there guys," Andy said to us. "Scott has something that he wants to tell your dad."

"Mr. Thumb, could you please come over here for a minute, sir." Andy said.

Andy was definitely all business here the way he was addressing Dad like that.

"Sure Andy, be there in a second." Dad got up from the bench on the end of the dock, leaving Mom and Polly sitting there, and walked over to us.

"What's up?" He asked.

"My brother has something that he wants to tell you, sir," Andy said.

Andy was looking Dad square in the eye. I had no idea what was going on, but with Scott squirming around uncomfortable as a minnow stuck on a fishhook, I have to admit, I sure was enjoying it.

"Tell him Scott, tell him now," Andy commanded.

"Mr. Thumb, I just want to let you know that it was an accident and that I didn't mean to do it."

"Scott, don't lie, don't fib, don't soft pedal it, you tell it straight or I'll whup you right now," Andy said as he gave his brother's arm a tighter squeeze and a bit of a shake.

"Do what?" Dad asked.

Realizing that he was completely trapped with no way out, Scott took a deep breath, and looking down at the tops of his shoes, he stammered out the words that I couldn't believe I was actually hearing.

"Mr. Thumb, at the range today, I was the one who shot Auggie's clothespin. I did it deliberately to break his pin, but I never meant to break the wire, I swear on that!"

If I'd been on the trampoline, I'd a done a back flip, but I just stood there and stayed quiet. Suddenly this had gone from being one of my worst days to being one of my best days. I couldn't believe how everything was working out.

"Scott, do your parents know this?" Dad asked him.

"Yessir."

"And what did they say about this?"

"They said that I have to pay for the damages, and my dad was going to talk to you about it later, once he and my mom got back from Mr. Miller's store."

"Well thank you for clearing that up for us, Scott. I appreciate you telling the truth. But you don't have to pay all the damages, Auggie will chip in as well."

What! Why the heck did I have to pay anything? This wasn't fair. I started to tell Dad no way am I paying one red cent when Timmy suddenly kicked me in the back of the leg.

"Shut up, Auggie. Just shut up," he whispered at me.

For once in my life, I listened to him and closed my mouth.

"Auggie will pay the twenty-five cents for the clothespin, and you will take responsibility for the cost of the wire repair," Dad told Scott.

As he said this, Dad struggled to keep his smile hidden, and looking over I saw Andy smile as well.

Twenty-five cents. Heck, I could live with that. I woulda paid twice that to see what I'd just seen happen with Scott, Andy, and Dad. Nobody deserved that more than Scotty Samuelson and all I had to do was just stand there and be quiet. What a bargain!

"Thank you, sir," Andy said to Dad.

At that, he let go of Scott and once free, Scott ran straight back to his cabin without saying another word to anyone. Polly walked down to join us and then she and Andy shuffled off down the beach.

Since the air was clearing so nicely, I took the opportunity to tell Dad all about what happened at the Miller's store with me wrestling Scott and him stealing the soda pop and everything. The whole time that I was telling Dad, he didn't say a word. He stood there taking it all in and at the end, with a bemused look on his face, he opened his arms and motioned me in for a hug. As he hugged me he said, "Auggie, I'm glad that you straightened everything out with Mr. Miller, and I'm proud of you for standing up to Scott, real proud. You weren't mean, you weren't trying to hurt him, you just knew that's what had to be done. Son, that's a sign of character, and a sign of being a man, well done."

When Dad said that to me, you coulda knocked me over with a feather. Dad had just complimented me on being a man and having character. Dad didn't throw those words around lightly, so hearing him tell me that made me love him all the more.

With that same half smile on his face, Dad looked from Timmy to David to me, and said, "Now, unless one of you boys has another surprise or story for me today, I'm going to go back and join your mother."

"No sir, that's all we've got." I said.

Dad turned and headed back down the dock towards Mom and I swear that I saw that smile on his face growing when he turned to go. Timmy, David and I just stood there watching as

Dad walked back down the dock to where Mom was sitting. As he walked away, I said, "I don't get it, why in the world would Scott fess up to something when he'd gotten clean away with it?"

"You really are an idiot, aren't you," Timmy said to me. "Open your eyes!"

"Huh, whaddya mean?"

"Who's Andy with right now?" Timmy asked me. "Just look."

I did look, and saw Andy with Polly, but I still didn't get it. "So?" I asked.

"So, Squirt, once I saw the targets, I knew that Scott must've shot your clothespin, but after thinking on it for a bit, I realized that without him confessing, there was no way that you could get Dad or Mr. Meyer to change their minds about it being you. So then I figured that the only one of us who could get Scott to fess up was Andy, and the only one who I thought could get Andy to actually lower the hammer on Scott is the person that he's currently holding hands with walking down the beach. So I just mentioned it to Polly after dinner, and she did all the rest."

"Holy cow, wow, thanks brother!"

Maybe Timmy actually was the smartest after all.

Chapter Thirteen

GOING TO WAR

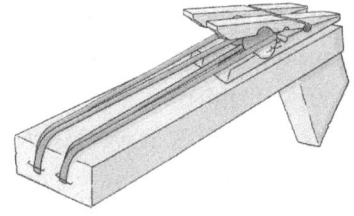

As soon as we got home from the lake I couldn't wait to head over to Uncle Alan's and check on Jake and the rest of the pups. That was all we really talked about on the ride home. Well that, and Dad did ask me to tell him once again about how it went with Scott and me at Mr. Miller's. I think that he just liked hearing how I'd come out on top and in his words, "acted very maturely" and with "great restraint" in getting Scott to admit the truth. I think it made him feel real proud of me. Honestly, I think that it also gave him a sense of satisfaction, since every time that we finished talking about it, he'd say, "And that's why I taught you boys how to wrestle."

Or, he'd ask rhetorically, "Aren't you glad that I taught you boys to wrestle?"

As soon as we unloaded the car and put everything away, all of us kids hightailed it over to Uncle Alan's. Even Polly came with us. I think that the only reason she came was that Mom had to make some phone calls so Polly's lifeline wouldn't be available to her for an hour or so. Anyway, I was sorta glad that Polly came with us. Ever since she bailed me out at the lake, I had a whole new appreciation for her.

The pups had grown quite a bit since we were last there. Uncle Alan was away at work, so it was just Aunt Joan and the kids. At first, when we saw the pups, we couldn't tell which one was Jake, as they all looked pretty much alike. David was the first one to recognize him and he shouted out, "There he is!"

He bent down, scooped him up and held him against his chest. The black splotch on Jake's face had given him away. We all crowded around him until Aunt Joan said,

"Kids, give him some room to play. You'll have plenty of time to give him your love soon enough."

"How much longer until we can take him home?" I asked.

"Well Auggie, depending on how he does, that's still a few weeks away. But remember, you kids can come over here whenever you like to see him. You'll just have to be patient."

A few weeks! I wanted him now! I didn't have enough time to be patient!

"Timmy, please give your mother this list of things that you'll need to have before you take Jake home, as you won't want to take him home until you've gotten them," she added.

"Yes ma'am," Timmy answered.

Aunt Joan handed him a list of all the items that we'd need to buy like dog food, bowls, a leash, a collar, and other things. I didn't realize dogs needed so much stuff.

After a bit, the pups were tired out and fell sound asleep. We made sure that Jake was fine and now that we were sure that he'd remembered all of us, we headed back home.

"Jake likes me the best," Timmy said smugly as soon as we left their house.

"Awwn't Aww! No way! Did you see how he came to me first right after David set him down?" I answered defiantly.

"No he didn't, he came to me first. You didn't even recognize him!" Timmy answered.

"I did too!"

"Would you two idiots shut up already," David said. "Auggie, he's trying to wind you up. Just ignore him."

"Why couldn't I've had sisters?" Polly asked sarcastically looking up and rolling her eyes. "At least one would've been an improvement! Like Katie for instance, she'd be a great little sister, right Auggie? You and she could've been twins!"

I couldn't believe it, now Polly was trying to wind me up. I think that I liked her better when she was glued to the phone in the kitchen. However, this time I refused to take the bait and decided to just break into a run and be the first one home. As I ran off towards our house, I could hear them all laughing. Maybe if I wasn't the youngest, I'da thought it was funny too.

The next couple of weeks seemed to drag by. The days were still hot and muggy; the dog days of summer Dad called them. Since Jake would be coming home soon, I thought that was an appropriate name for them. However, Dad explained that the term didn't really have anything to do with dogs, but that it was tied to some ancient Greek or Roman thing about a dog star rising and setting with the sun. Lots of the time I'd only half listen when Dad was trying to impart some useless knowledge to us. Greek and Roman mythology, I'd be getting plenty of that in school soon enough so I didn't really hear all the rest of what he said. I just decided that for now, as far as I was concerned, the expression was based on the fact that during these days even dogs thought it was too hot to do anything other than lay around in the shade.

On one of these dog days, Timmy, David and I were sitting in the morning shade on the back stoop and I started telling my brothers about how much fun it would be to train Jake for hunting especially with Dad and Uncle Alan helping us.

"I don't know Auggie, I know you're super excited about going bird hunting and everything, but heck none of us even have shotguns," David said.

"Yeah, David, but we can ask Mom and Dad to get them for us to be our early birthday presents this year."

"I dunno, Auggie, and besides that, Dad's even told us that it's been years since he's hunted."

"So what, he can start up again with Uncle Howard and Uncle Alan."

Auggie, none of us even know the first thing about training a hunting dog," Timmy said. "And with our luck, we'll probably have him pointing the garbage can instead of pheasants."

"Real funny! I can't believe you guys are backing out now!"

"We're not backing out, Squirt, it's just that once football starts that's where my focus is going to be," David said.

"Well now don't go telling Mom and Dad that, or they'll change their minds about letting us get Jake."

Don't be a dope, Auggie. We're not gonna go tell 'em that we're not gonna do anything for Jake. We want to get him too, so we'll be there to do all the chores with him, it's just that with football, David and me ain't gonna have the time to train him for hunting." Timmy explained.

"Okay, suit yourselves, but I'm still gonna train him for hunting!"

I was starting to get sore, but it was pointless to keep arguing with them since I knew that I wasn't gonna change their minds. Besides, the more I thought about it, the more I figured that with Uncle Alan's help, Dad and I'd train Jake to hunt, and once they saw how much fun it was, they'd probably want to do it too.

"Well, I know that once I've got him trained, Dad'll let me get a shotgun and I'll be hunting with him and Uncle Howard and Uncle Alan every weekend, while you guys are being tacklin' dummies on a football field somewhere!" I whined to my brothers, still a little sore about the whole thing.

"And here I was thinking that you were getting all mature and everything Auggie," Timmy said.

"Look little brother, don't take it so personal and get yourself all worked up over it. Relax. Train Jake, and when we're around we'll help you, and besides, you're getting kinda far ahead of yourself, since none of us even have BB guns!" David said.

David was right. Mom had never been big on any of us having a BB gun. While she never out and out told us no, I think that she was just worried we'd end up shooting each other in the eye and we'd all be walking around the house blind or something. However, whenever I brought it up to Dad, all he'd ever say was, "Save your nickels!"

That was Dad's answer to almost any request that we made to him to get something. Although, this time, I had taken him literally. I had a big jar full of not only nickels, but also dimes, quarters, and any other change that I could get along with the money earned from my paper route, which I was saving to get a BB gun. Unfortunately, this stash of cash had taken a big hit when I had to replace Timmy's aquarium fish, but luckily, it had been spared being completely wiped out by Scott fessing up at the lake, so I almost had what I needed to buy a BB gun.

Talking about shotguns and BB guns got me thinking about a "gun" that was no problem to get, and that was a rubber band gun. With that thought in my mind I blurted out, "Let's make rubber band guns!"

"No, those are stupid," Timmy replied. "I don't wanna do that."

"Neither do I," David said.

"Okay, well if you guys want to be boring, then I'm gonna see if Dean's out and if he wants to make 'em then."

I got up, and with my right hand smacked what little dust had accumulated on the backside of my jeans and headed over to Dean's house. When I got there he had just finished cleaning out their garage and was sweeping their patio.

"Hey Dean, whatcha doing?"

"What's it look like Auggie?" He replied with a laugh. "I just have to finish the patio and then I can go do something."

"Do ya wanna make rubber band guns?"

"Yeah that'd be fun," He answered.

"If we make them, then I bet we can get my brothers to make them too. And if they join in, then we can have a better war."

We made our rubber band guns by taking a chunk of two by four, about twelve inches long, stapling one of those thick rubber bands to its front and then nailing a clothespin to its back. You also nailed a smaller piece of wood to the bottom of the two by four to function as the grip. We always made ours double-barreled by stapling two rubber bands side by side on the front and nailing two clothespins side by side on the back. These clothespins were the pincher type made with two pieces of wood with a spring hinge in the middle that you could open and close.

Dean and I went downstairs into his parents' basement to find the necessary materials, and within a manner of minutes had our finely crafted weapons ready to engage in battle. Now we just needed some worthy opponents to make it full-scale war.

Sure enough, when we walked back to our house David and Timmy wanted to play as well. They quickly went downstairs to make their guns. While they were making their guns, Dean and I got our ammo. Our ammo consisted of little green crab apples that we pulled from the Nolan's tree in their side yard. It was a big tree that had thousands of crab apples on it. Crab apples are small and round about the size of a pea, and the green ones are hard and fit perfectly into the opening in the jaws of the clothespin. The clothespin's opening was to grip the clothesline, but in this case, it gripped the crab apple.

In order to operate a rubber band gun, you put the crab apple inside one of the rubber bands, then, with your thumb and forefinger holding the end of the rubber band around the crab apple, you stretched the band all the way back towards the open jaw of the clothespin. Once you had the crab apple positioned in the rounded out bit of the clothespin you eased the pressure off the back of the clothespin, closing it on the crab apple. Do this twice, and your double-barreled rubber band gun was fully locked and loaded.

"I bet you can't hit that post," Dean challenged, pointing to the speed limit sign on the side of the street.

"First one to hit it wins," I said.

My first shot sailed wide to the left, and Dean's first shot went wide right. I took careful aim with my second shot and ba-ping, I nailed it right in its center.

"Top that, Nolan!"

With his second shot, Dean hit it as well so now we were tied.

While we were reloading, Timmy and David came out with their newly made guns. As soon as they saw us shooting ours, they immediately started over to the Nolan's tree to pick their ammo. With our pockets jammed full of crab apples, Dean and I looked at each other and in silent agreement as soon as we had our guns loaded, we both shot at my brothers.

"Oww! You idiot!" Timmy said as my shot hit him in the thigh. "I'm not ready yet!"

"Too bad!" Dean yelled as he fired at David.

Now that they'd both been hit, they took off running like crazy for the Nolan's tree to get ammo to get us back. Meanwhile Dean and I reloaded and set off in hot pursuit. Dean was getting ahead of me, and I realized that I wouldn't get to my brothers before they got to the tree, so seeing how I had a good shot, I squeezed the left side pin on my gun and shot Dean squarely in the back.

"Oww! What was that for? We're on the same team, you idiot!" Dean screeched as he slammed on his brakes and turned to face me.

"There's no teams!" I yelled as I loosed my second barrel at him.

My shot flew out errantly and whizzed harmlessly past him.

"You're out of ammo, Squirt!" he laughed.

Realizing that, I spun around and running in a zigzag pattern tried to get away without being shot.

Blam! The shot hit me right in the back of the head.

"Oww!" I wailed. "You got me, you got me! Uncle, uncle, timeout!"

Dean just laughed.

"Serves you right, Thumb. That was a dirty trick shooting me in the back."

"Okay, okay, but I couldn't help it, you were too good of a target."

Distracted as we were with our own injuries, we'd momentarily forgotten about Timmy and David, but they hadn't forgotten about us. Now fully armed, and with loaded guns, they came running at us and before we could even move or much less reload, they were upon us and let fly with both barrels. I got hit twice and Dean once.

"Uncle, uncle, timeout!" I cried again. "Stop, stop!"

Timmy and David were laughing.

"David, awesome shot bro! You got him right in the chest!" Timmy exclaimed.

"No more, no more!" Dean said. "If we keep this up one of us is going to get hit in the eye."

"Get hit in the eye," that was our default way to honorably end the war. It wasn't cowardice or fear of getting shot, it was purely simple concern for the safety of all of us. That and the knowledge that if one of us shot another one's eye out, we'd never hear the end of it, and we'd probably never ever get to make rubber band guns again.

Chapter Fourteen

Jake

AND JUST LIKE THAT, summer was essentially over. Now don't get me wrong, school hadn't started yet, that was still a few days away. No, what had happened was Mom corralled us boys into going "school shopping." None of us liked it. Not at all. Not one single bit, but we had no choice. We really hated it because it meant giving up one of our last summer days to spend it stuck in the mall trying on all kinds of nice clothes and stuff that we'd only wear for school.

Polly didn't have to go as she had already gone with her friends and besides, even if she did, she wouldn't mind, since she actually liked to go shopping. With Polly, shopping came in a close second to talking on the phone, so absolutely no issue for her. The main reason that she turned down the opportunity to go to the mall, was that we'd be there as well. The thought of having all three of us moaning and complaining about trying on dress pants, starched shirts and leather shoes was just too much for her to bear, so she opted out. The fact that the phone would be free for the whole time that we were gone probably didn't even enter into her thinking at all. Yeah, probably.

The dreaded trip to the mall wasn't as bad as I originally thought. We all just agreed to the first things that Mom brought us, and with that level of cooperation, we were out of there in record time.

When we got home from the mall, we got great news. Polly told us that Aunt Joan had called and told us that we could pick up Jake anytime now. How Aunt Joan got through on the phone line is beyond me. It must've been one of those rare moments when Polly had to hang it up and let it cool down to room temperature! Since Mom had kept the car to take us shopping, Dad was coming home on the bus and I made sure that I was at the stop waiting for him when the bus pulled up.

With the news that we could now get Jake, there was no holding back. As soon as Dad stepped off the bus, I let him have it.

"Dad, Aunt Joan says that we can pick up Jake now! Can we go get him now, please, can we?"

"Whoa there boy! Slow down!" he said chuckling.

"Just before I left work, your mother called and told me the news, so I knew this was coming. Let's walk home and you can tell me all about your day, and then after supper we can go get your pup."

Timmy and David were just getting home from football practice when Dad and I walked up our drive. They would be in the eighth grade once school officially started, and this was their second season of playing football since our school's program started in the seventh grade. However, all of us had several years of backyard football experience under our belts, so we considered ourselves pretty good football players. Since I was only going into sixth grade, I still had to wait a year before I could tryout.

"How'd practice go, boys?" Dad asked them.

"It was okay. We ran a lot, did pushups and sit-ups, and had to get timed in the 40 yard dash." Timmy answered.

"These first couple of days are nothing but conditioning and other drills so it'll be a few more days before we start doing actual football stuff," added David.

David had been a linebacker last year and was hoping to play that position this year as well, and Timmy was hoping to continue as a wide receiver but the coach had said no positions were guaranteed, and so they wouldn't find out what positions they'd be playing until the end of the week.

We all ate as fast as we could, well, all of us except Dad that is. He took his time eating and dragged it out by asking us a bunch of questions. He just liked torturing us and watching us squirm impatiently in our seats wanting to get over to Uncle Alan's house. Finally, Mom had to step in and take charge.

"Alright kids, clear the table, clean up the kitchen, put everything away, and then we'll head over to get Jake. If your father's still eating when we're ready to go, then he can just see Jake when we bring him home."

Mom had a way with words. Whenever she was talking to us in front of Dad and referred to him as "your father," she was letting him know that whatever he was doing was either silly or just way too much and that he should stop doing it. When she used the term "your father" she would tilt her head towards him, raise her eyebrows and say it with a knowing smile on her face. It worked every time.

"Okay, okay, let's get going! Who's going to be the last one in the car?" Dad called out trying to make it sound like he was the one that was the most eager to go, and that it was the rest of us making him late.

We all piled into the car and Dad drove over to Uncle Alan's house. Jake was now ten weeks old and a rambunctious little puppy with needle sharp teeth. He would mouth anything that got in front of him so it was always best to have a chew toy in your hands to keep him occupied.

"Remember, he's not housebroken yet, so be prepared to take him out every time as soon as he wakes up and whenever he finishes either drinking or eating," Aunt Joan told us. "And even with that, you'll probably still have accidents in the house."

She told us a lot of other things too, but I don't think anyone other than Mom and Dad was actually listening, all of us were just too excited to pay attention. We just nodded our heads, said, "Yes Ma'am," and agreed to everything she was saying while we played with Jake.

It was a little after eight o'clock in the evening when we got home. Polly held him in her lap during the drive back, and when we got out of the car, she set him down in the front yard.

"Let him run around a bit and get some exercise before we bring him in," Dad said to all of us.

"Okay," I replied.

We played with him in the yard with a ball and some dog toys until he seemed to lose interest.

"Jake just peed, so let's bring him in now," Timmy said.

David got to him before I could, and he picked him up, carried him inside and set him down in the kitchen.

The kitchen was to be Jake's new home. We copied what Uncle Alan and Aunt Joan had done for Nellie and put an old blanket in a large cardboard box with the front cut down and set this up in the corner of our kitchen. We then spread some newspapers on the floor in case he had to pee or poop. The kitchen floor was tile, so if he missed the newspapers, cleanups wouldn't be too tough. We could close off the end of the kitchen nearest his box with the sliding pocket door that separated it from the dining room, and to block the other end, Dad had cut a section of plywood that we braced against the entryway into the living room. In this way Jake would have the whole kitchen to himself whenever we were gone or asleep at night.

When we all came in, Dad put the plywood up against the entryway into the living room while we stayed in the kitchen playing with Jake and watching him explore his new home.

"I've got my route then practice in the morning, so I'm going to bed now," David said.

"Me too," added Timmy.

They had two-a-day practices for these first few days before school started, so their minds were more on football then on puppies.

"I have practice tomorrow morning too, so I'll call it a night as well," said Polly.

Polly ran cross-country on her high school team and they were in the middle of their two-a-day practices. Since school wouldn't start for another three days, I was the only one without a wake-up call. I stayed in the kitchen sitting on the floor with Jake on my lap nibbling on my hands and fingers while I pet him.

"August, time for bed," Dad called out to me from the living room. "Make sure that the board is secure, blocking the living room and close the door behind you as you leave the kitchen," he added.

"Okay."

I got up slowly and set a sleeping Jake down in his box on his blanket, turned out the kitchen light and slid the door shut. I tiptoed back to my room, changed into my pajamas and slid into bed. I couldn't believe it. We had a dog. All I could think about as I drifted off to sleep was him and me hunting pheasants in a field. Jake locked in a point; nose out forward, front leg up and bent, his tail straight out, and me standing behind him with my shotgun at the ready waiting for the bird to flush.

"Arrroooohhh!"

The cry was followed by a couple of yips and yelps.

I was startled awake. So were Timmy and David.

"What time is it?" David asked groggily.

He turned on his flashlight and looked at his alarm clock. It was just past eleven o'clock.

"Arrroooohhh! Arrff, arrff!"

I remember Aunt Joan telling us that he might cry the first couple of nights, but that if we ignored him, he'd eventually settle down and go back to sleep. I got up anyway just to check and make sure that he was all right but as I came into the dining room and approached the sliding kitchen door, Dad was already there standing in front of it and had the door pulled shut.

"I figured that one of you would get out of bed and try to comfort him," Dad whispered to me. "Auggie, you can't do that or he'll never stop whining, so go back to bed."

"Dad, are you sure? What if he's hurt?"

"He's not hurt, he's just lonely. He's used to sleeping at Alan and Joan's with Nellie and his brothers and sisters, so right now he's a little bit scared. Once he gets used to our house as his new home this will stop. Now back to bed with you."

Reluctantly I went back to our room to go to bed.

"Close the door." David grumpily told me.

I pushed our room door closed but even with it closed, we could plainly hear Jake alternately crying and barking in the kitchen. Then all of a sudden, we heard a loud crash.

KABAMMM!

I sprang from my bed, grabbed my robe, and ran out to the kitchen. Jake was nowhere to be seen. I rounded the corner to the other end of the kitchen and saw Dad's handcrafted plywood barricade laying on the floor. Oh no! Then in the darkness, I thought that I could hear water running. The hall light switched on, and Dad was standing at the other end of the living room in the hallway that led to my parents' bedroom and he did not look happy.

"Auggie, get that dog out of the living room and get that mess cleaned up now!"

The water that was running wasn't water, and it was in a puddle on the living room carpet. I scooped Jake up and headed to the back door. Cradling him in one arm, I opened the door, took him out and set him down in the yard. All he did was walk around and sniff stuff. He'd already peed all over the living room, so he didn't have to go again. It was midnight, and even though everyone was awake, I was the only one not in bed. I brought Jake in and set him down in the kitchen. I got paper towels and some cleaner and went into the living room to start scrubbing the pee spot. Jake came up to the barricade and started whining. Dad had braced it better with a chair so it wouldn't fall over again and Jake couldn't get out.

"Sssshh, boy, you'll wake everyone up again."

After a few dabs and scrubs I figured the living room rug was clean enough, so I headed into the kitchen to put Jake back in his bed. However, he didn't want to sleep, he wanted to play. I turned the kitchen light off, and laid down on the floor with my arm in his box and let him lie next to me. As soon as he fell asleep, I'd go back to bed.

"Auggie, what are you doing? Have you been out here all night?" David quietly asked as he nudged me awake with his foot. "You idiot, if Dad finds out that you slept all night on the kitchen floor, you're gonna be in trouble."

It was four thirty in the morning and David and Timmy were up to go deliver their paper routes.

"You go back to bed now and I'll take him out to pee in the backyard, bring him in, and make sure that he's in his box. Then I'm leaving." Timmy said to me.

"Okay, thanks Timmy, but what if he keeps crying?"

"Just ignore him," they both answered in unison.

I went back to bed and Timmy brought Jake in, put him in the kitchen, and left to go deliver his route.

By some miracle, Jake didn't cry and I must've fallen asleep because the next thing I knew I heard Dad calling my name and telling me to take Jake out. It was six thirty, Dad's regular time to get up for work, and everything seemed normal.

"Did you have a good sleep, my boy?" Dad asked me all cheerful like. He asked in a way that made me think he already knew the answer to his question.

I was absolutely exhausted, but no way was I going to admit that to Dad. As it was, I really had to get this figured out quickly or soon I'd be asking him to get another box and blanket to put in the kitchen for me!

Chapter Fifteen

THE RACE

WE ONLY HAD ONE more sleepless night, then after that Jake got used to his new home and settled into a routine. School started that Monday and with Timmy, David and Polly at practice every day after school it fell to me to train Jake. Mom was great with him during the day taking him out every hour or so, making him sit and stay, and giving him lots of pets and love. I also couldn't help but notice that Dad was playing with him more and more after work as well. One evening after supper, Dad had pulled Jake up and set him on his lap while he sat outside and read his newspaper.

"Hey Dad, if Jake cries tonight, will you go sleep in the kitchen with him?" I laughed as I teased him. "Just so you know, you look more comfortable with him in your lap than he does!"

Dad just laughed, gave Jake a pat and set him down saying, "Show me what he's learned so far."

"Okay. Jake come!" I called.

Jake came bounding over to me and I gave him a treat.

"Good boy, Jake, good boy!" I said as I pet him and scratched under his chin.

He loved the attention. I then made him sit and stay, and after he did that, I slowly backed away from him, called him again, and he came running up to me. I repeated this two more times only giving him a treat every other time, but giving him love and attention every time.

"Uncle Alan told me not to give him a treat every time, but to always give him love so that eventually we can wean him from the treats and he'll do it just for love."

"That sounds like great advice, my boy, and it sure looks to be working! Keep at it and be patient, and you'll have a great dog." Dad added.

"Honey, I have a list of things that we need from the store, if you wouldn't mind getting them for me," Mom called out to Dad.

"Be there in a minute, Hun."

Dad went inside to learn what Mom's assignment for him was, and I stayed outside with Jake. Polly came outside and joined me and we both took turns giving Jake commands and treats. Polly's birthday was this coming Saturday, and even though she was turning seventeen, Mom still wanted to have a party for her. It was fun watching the two of them go at it. Polly trying to tell Mom that she was seventeen and too old for a party, and Mom telling her that she would always be "her baby." Polly didn't stand a chance. Mom did make some concessions though. No more pin-the-tail-on-the-donkey games or bobbing for apples, but she absolutely would have some balloons and a cake.

"Polly, are you inviting any of your friends over for your birthday party?" I asked trying to wind her up.

"No, little brother, it will just be us." Polly answered, not taking the bait at all. "Besides, I like it when Mom makes a fuss over us, it'll be fun."

Saturday morning dawned bright and sunny. It was going to be a busy day. Polly had a cross-country meet at ten in the morning, and Timmy and David had a football game starting at noon. One of Polly's teammates picked her up a little before nine and Mom told her that she, Dad and I would be there to cheer her on shortly.

"Dad, can we take Jake with us to Polly's meet and to the boys' game?" I asked.

"Sure, but you need to watch him very closely and make sure that he doesn't cause any trouble," Dad replied.

"I know, I know, he'll be good," I promised.

Dad shot me a glance when I answered with "I know" since it wasn't the most respectful response. Realizing that I'd been disrespectful and a little too impatient in my answer, I quickly added, "Yessir, I'll make sure that he behaves."

There were already tons of people at the meet when we arrived. This was a big meet with several high school teams participating. A local country club was hosting the meet and the hilly course went in and out of patches of woods ending in a flat straight away stretch of fifty yards or so. I kept a firm grip on Jake's leash and stood by Mom and Dad. People kept coming up to Jake and telling me how cute he was and asking me all kinds of questions about how old he was, what kind of dog he was, and what his name was. Jake loved all the attention, and it was good to have him around people.

"The race is starting, so Mom and I are going over to the starting line to see Polly better," Dad told me. "You stay here with Jake, since it'll be pretty crowded over there."

"Okay, I'll probably just work some commands with him."

They moved off to the starting line with all the other spectators and Jake and I were by ourselves. Since no one else was around, I unclipped his leash so that I could practice "come" with him. He'd been doing it really well lately and I was in a bit of a "show-off" mood. While I wanted everyone to see how great a dog he was, I really wanted to show off how great a dog trainer I was.

"BAM!" The gun sounded and the race started. The sound of the gun startled me and I looked up and saw a whole pack of high school girls moving out over the course. They were about a quarter of a mile away and heading into the first patch of woods. I turned back to Jake, except – he wasn't there! I couldn't believe it! I'd only looked away for a couple of seconds when the gun sounded, and I'd told him to sit and stay and now I couldn't find him.

"Jake come! Jake come!" I called out frantically.

I looked all around. I couldn't see him. How in the heck could he have gotten so far away? This was a disaster! A feeling of immense panic overwhelmed me. I felt like I'd just been punched in the stomach. How could I have lost my dog? Where could he have gone?

"Jake come! Jake come! Here boy!"

Nothing. No sight of him. Mom and Dad would be coming back any minute now, and I would be in big trouble if I didn't have Jake. He must've gone into the woods. I ran in there and continued to call his name.

"Jake come! Jake come!"

The girls were in the last patch of woods before the final turn onto the fifty yard straightaway. Spectators were standing on both sides of the trail just on the outside of the woods, crowding up to the edges trying to see the runners. I was in the woods running around not sure which way to go when I caught a glimpse of him running towards all the girls racing.

OH NO!

I had to get to him before he got trampled. Polly was in the front group of girls and had no idea that Jake was loose and chasing her. I had no choice. I had to catch Jake! I took off sprinting after him, but it was too late. He broke out of the woods and quickly gained ground on Polly. People started laughing and pointing at Jake. He was running right alongside the girls as if he was in the race! And unfortunately, so was I!

There was no way I was hiding this one. I came out of the woods on the final turn, running in my Red Ball Jets canvas sneakers leash in hand. Jake was just in front of me, but I couldn't catch him. Mom and Dad had been watching Polly run by when they suddenly saw Jake pass them, and then in unison, they turned back and saw me run past them towards Jake. Mom's hand came up to her mouth in shocked disbelief and Dad's eyes almost bulged completely out of his head! Up ahead I saw that Jake had come to a stop just past the finish line when he got to Polly. Unfortunately, I had already entered the funnel that they had roped off to keep spectators out and to ensure the correct order for the finishers so I had no choice but to keep going and cross the finish line.

What a dope! People were laughing and shaking their heads at me. A race official shouted at me to get out of the way, but the only way that I could go was in the same direction as the runners, so I kept moving forward with them. I never felt stupider in my life. Polly was now holding Jake and I thought for sure that she'd be mad at me. However, she was actually smiling. The only reason that I could think of was that Jake hadn't interfered with anyone and it wasn't until after she crossed the finish line that he came up to her. Also, several girls crowded around her trying to pet Jake.

"Auggie, give me his leash and I'll take him from here," Polly told me. "Besides little brother, I'm guessing that Mom and Dad are going to want to talk to you!"

There was nothing I could say. I handed her the leash and as I made my way out of the finish area I could feel everyone's eyes just burning holes in me. If only I hadn't left my cloak of invisibility at home!

"August Thumb, come over here right now!" Mom wasted no time in calling me out.

"What in tarnation happened?" Dad demanded.

I started to explain, but no words would come out, nor would any do it justice.

"I think that I'll be holding the leash at the boy's game," Mom said sternly.

"I just have one question for you," Dad said.

"Yessir," I answered sheepishly.

Laughingly he asked, "What place did you end up getting?"

Chapter Sixteen

BALLOONS

WHEN WE GOT TO their game, Timmy and David were out on the field warming up with the rest of the team and true to her word, Mom was holding Jake's leash. I think she checked to make sure everything was secure at least twenty times in the first five minutes we were at the field. We couldn't go into the bleachers with Jake, so we stood against the fence alongside the field to watch. I wish that I could talk about how great the game was and how well my brothers played, but all I could think about was how stupid I'd been with Jake and so I didn't really pay attention to the game. I still couldn't believe it, my first outing with him, and I almost ruined a high school cross-country race! Although Dad did make me laugh when he asked what place I got, I knew that from now on, I would have to do better with Jake if I wanted to keep taking him places.

The boys won their game by a score of fourteen to seven and once the team finished their post-game chat, Timmy and David came over to us.

"Great game boys!" Dad said. "Timmy, great catch in the end zone for that touchdown, and David, you had some great tackles out there!"

"Thanks, Dad!" They both answered.

"I thought you boys looked so big, strong and handsome in your uniforms," Mom remarked.

Timmy and David just looked at each other and smiled at what Mom had said. Mom's comment was just such a typical "Mom comment."

"Now before we get home, we've got to stop at the store so that I can run in and get a few things for Polly's party today," Mom said.

We got to the store, and Mom went inside and picked up some helium filled balloons and a fancy cake that she had ordered. You'd think by the way Mom was acting Polly was turning seven, not seventeen!

We got home, and while Timmy and David unloaded the car, I took Jake into the backyard to let him do his business. Polly was already home, and she smiled when she saw the balloons.

"Mom, are we having a clown and a waterslide as well?" Polly asked cracking herself up.

"Very funny, sweetheart," Mom replied. "You're still my baby and there's nothing wrong with having a few balloons to make it more festive, and besides, who doesn't like balloons?"

"Sure Mom, whatever you say!" Polly laughed as she headed to her room to change.

Mom had gotten four balloons, one for each of us she said. This made us laugh since we all thought that we were too old for balloons. Dad just smiled and took it all in stride.

The "party" was more than likely just going to be us eating cake after supper and singing "Happy Birthday" to Polly anyway, so the balloons weren't really all that central to the event, they were just a way for Mom to have some fun. So until Polly's big event, the balloons just floated along aimlessly in the living room bumping along the ceiling waiting for the call of the party.

After Timmy and David had changed and we'd eaten lunch, my brothers and I took Jake outside and we sat around playing with him and talking about the day's events. Timmy and David kept reminding me about how much of an idiot I'd been at the meet and saying that they wished they could've been there to see me chasing after Jake and almost messing up a race. Thankfully, Dean came over so I tried to switch the topic to talk about something else. However, before I could get a word out, David relayed the whole story to Dean.

"Auggie, that's spectacular! I would've paid hard-earned cash money to see that!" Dean exclaimed laughingly.

"Really? Now I need to hear this from you as well? Gimmie a break!" I added.

"Oh lighten up Auggie, you've gotta admit, it's pretty funny!" Dean replied.

"Yeah, I know, but I'm just not gonna admit that now."

Dad and Mom came outside and Dad had Jake's leash in his hand.

"Well hello there, Mr. Nolan!" Dad said cheerfully when he saw Dean. "Did August tell you what place he got in Polly's race today?"

Dad was never one to miss an opportunity to make a joke.

"No sir. I heard that he and Jake were running around in the woods and stuff, but he didn't tell me that they counted his finish. Turning to me Dean said, "Hey, what place did you get Auggie?" Dean couldn't help himself and laughed as he asked me.

"Uggh," was all I could muster as I shook my head at him.

Dad laughed and said, "Your mom and I are going to take Jake for a walk round the block." He called Jake over, clipped his leash on him and they headed down the driveway towards our sidewalk.

Once Dad and Mom left, I threw the football that I was holding at Dean and we started playing catch. Timmy and David joined in and we got a game of two-on-two backyard football going. When Mom and Dad came back, Mom set about getting everything ready for supper. After a while Dean headed home and once everything was ready, Dad cooked burgers on the grill. We ate outside enjoying the warm fall evening. Afterwards we had the cake and ice cream and sang

"Happy Birthday" to Polly while the four balloons apparently forgotten, continued to just bump lazily along our living room ceiling whenever a bit of breeze came up.

Sunday morning dawned cloudy and rainy. After I finished delivering my paper route, I went back to bed until Dad woke me up to get ready for Mass. When we got home, there wasn't much to do, as the ground was all wet and it was still spitting rain. Polly borrowed the car and took Jake over to her friend's house to show him off, Timmy and David started doing their homework, Mom was getting Sunday dinner ready, and Dad went out to the garage to fix something. I had to read a couple of chapters in my history book for school, but I just wasn't in the mood for it, so I had to figure out something else to do. Dean had gone somewhere with his dad and wouldn't be home for a while, so I was on my own to come up with an alternative to homework. It was then that I spied the balloon. It was suspended a few inches off the floor up against the living room wall held down by the weight of the string tied to its bottom.

Overnight, enough of the helium had leaked out of the balloons so that they were no longer able to float with their strings all the way up to the ceiling. They were only able to hold up about six or eight inches of string, so that's all the higher they were. Floating like this a few inches above the floor made them perfect targets – now I just needed a way to pop them. I found the other three balloons and bunched them all together. As I sat there pondering a fun way to pop these I suddenly remembered that in school, my friends and I would make slingshots by looping a rubber band around our thumb and forefinger and stretching it out as far as we could. Then we'd twist up a small piece of paper to make it thick, fold it in half over the stretched out rubber band, pull it back and let the paper fly. We'd shoot these at each other in class when the teacher wasn't looking. As long as we didn't hit them with any errant shots, the girls wouldn't tell on us. They usually just sighed and shook their heads at how silly and immature we were.

I rummaged through Mom's odds and ends drawer next to the refrigerator and found a fat rubber band that would be perfect for my slingshot, and right next to the rubber band I found a new yellow pencil. That pencil would be my arrow, and the rubber band would be my bow! This would work way better than folded paper!

To shoot the arrow correctly, once the rubber band was stretched out, I'd put the eraser end of the pencil against one side of the rubber band, centered in the middle, hold it with the thumb and forefinger of my other hand, pull it back, resting the shaft of the pencil against the other side of the rubber band, aim, and let it fly. This would be awesome!

Obviously, I needed to sharpen the pencil. No self-respecting archer goes into battle without sharp arrows, and if the pencil wasn't sharp, it'd just bounce off the balloon and what fun would that be? Turning the crank on the pencil sharpener which Dad had mounted on the wall inside the basement stairway, I honed the pencil tip to a razor sharp point. When the grinding wheels stopped removing material I quit turning the crank, pulled the pencil out, blew off the chips, and smoothed the long black point between my fingers. Heck, looking at it,

I figured that with the right shot it could bring down a grizzly bear! Bears aside, for now a balloon would have to suffice.

I sat on the living room floor about five feet away from the nearest balloon. I stretched the rubber band out between the forefinger and thumb of my left hand, placed the eraser end of the pencil against the one strand of the rubber band, centered it, pulled it as far back as it would go, rested it against the other strand, took careful aim, and let it fly.

"Augghh! Uummmhh! Oww, oww, oww!" The pencil hit the knuckle joint of my middle finger! What the heck? You've gotta be kidding me! Did I just shoot myself? At first, I didn't think that much of it since the pencil bounced off my finger and hit the floor, and when I looked at my finger there was barely any blood visible. However my knuckle was swelling up and starting to hurt.

Mannnnn, I couldn't believe that I'd just done that. When I flexed my finger, my knuckle didn't move much and it hurt. Looking around I found the pencil laying on the floor. I picked it up and noticed that the tip was missing. I assumed that it must've broken off when it hit the floor. I carried the pencil back into the kitchen and put it and the rubber band back in Mom's drawer. Might as well hide the evidence.

Man oh man, how stupid was I? My finger throbbed. I could see a black mark on my finger with a little drop of blood on it, and the knuckle was swollen, but that was it. I must've just bruised it. I figured that if the tip had broken off and stuck in my finger I'd be able to see it, and since I couldn't, I'd probably be all right. Now that I had a hurt finger and a broken arrow, I decided to abandon the great balloon shoot and find something else to do.

My finger hurt the rest of the day, but I figured that it would get better, and seeing how I didn't want to have to explain how it happened to anyone, I just kept it to myself. Unfortunately, the next morning when I woke up I could barely move my finger. It was really red and swollen. I had no choice, I had to show Mom, and so I headed into the kitchen.

"Mom, my finger hurts!"

"Auggie, let's see it. Auggie, what on earth happened?"

"I dunno."

"August Thumb! What did you do?"

"I accidentally hit it with a pencil."

What do you mean; you accidentally hit it with a pencil?"

"Well, I was trying to pop one of the balloons, and the pencil slipped and hit my finger right there."

"August, you are making no sense at all! Please tell me start to finish, everything that you were doing when you got hurt, and tell me now!"

I had to figure out how to explain it so that I didn't look like a complete moron. But, how do I describe shooting my finger with a razor sharp pencil, which I was using as an arrow with a rubber band bow to pop a balloon, and make it sound intelligent? Well if not intelligent, at least not unbelievably stupid. I gave up. There was no way that this was going to sound even remotely smart, so I just told her the truth.

"Auggie that is the silliest thing that I've ever heard." Turning my hand over and back, Mom gave it a thorough examination.

"Your knuckle is red, and swollen up quite a bit, so I can't tell if that's just because of the trauma, or if it's infected. Does it hurt to touch it?" Mom asked while she simultaneously touched my knuckle.

"Oww, ouch!" I yelped.

"Well I guess it does then." Mom said in that oh so perfect "Mom voice."

Why do moms always ask whether or not something hurts right at the moment that they're touching the injury? Why can't they ask the question, then wait for the answer before they try to touch it. I wish I knew.

"What's going on here? August, what did you do now?" Dad asked as he walked into the kitchen.

Before I could answer "nothing," Timmy and David came into the kitchen followed by Polly. I just sat there and didn't say anything. I let Mom tell everyone. The good thing is that everyone was there together, so I wouldn't have to sit through four retellings of the story.

Timmy, David and Polly burst out laughing.

"Auggie, you dope!" Timmy remarked.

"You really are a dope," David added.

"Boys, that'll be enough. Now go finish getting yourselves ready for school," Mom said.

"What do you think we should do, honey?" Dad asked.

Dad always deferred to Mom on any issue of injury or health with us.

"I don't know, but it looks like it could be infected, so I think that I should take him to Dr. Waggoner."

Dr. Waggoner was our pediatrician. He was super friendly, always wore a colorful shirt and tie, and called me Mr. Thumb, saying it in a cheerful voice with a big smile on his face. When we were little we got to pick toys out of his toy chest after our visits, but I hadn't done that for a few years now.

With me in the backseat moaning about how stupid I'd been, Mom drove Dad to his office, and after dropping him off, we went to see Dr. Waggoner.

"Mom, don't tell him how it happened, please."

"Auggie, he has to know what happened so that he knows what he's dealing with."

"Well can't you just tell him that I poked my finger with a pencil? You don't need to go into all the details about the rubber band and the balloon and stuff, do you?"

"Okay, I won't give him all the gory details, I'll tell him that you poked your finger with a pencil and that we think it might be infected."

"Thanks Mom!"

"Mr. Thumb, what do we have here?" Dr. Waggoner asked in his booming voice as he walked into the exam room.

"I hurt my finger with a pencil."

"Were you gripping it too tightly when you were writing out your math homework?" He joked.

"No, actually I was trying to pop a balloon."

The answer was out of me before I even realized what I'd said.

"Pop a balloon? That sounds exciting! I'd love to hear what happened!"

And with that, I relayed the entire story to Dr. Waggoner. He sat there holding my hand in his, slowly turning it over and looking closely at my knuckle.

"Mr. Thumb, we're going to send you down the hall to get an X-ray of your knuckle so we can see if there's anything in there that's causing you these problems."

"Okay. What's that like? I've never had an X-ray before."

"They're going to sit you in a chair, drop a heavy lead vest on you as a shield, have you put your hand on a table, and then pull a big thing that looks like a camera down to take a picture of your hand. They'll take a couple of pictures, and that'll be it. Afterwards, you and your mom will go to the waiting room while they develop the film. Once I get the pictures, I'll bring you back into our room to show you what's up."

After the X-ray, Mom and I were sitting in the waiting room when Dr. Waggoner called us to come back into the exam room. He had the X-ray picture stuck up on the light display and pointed to a small bright white spec that showed up on the knuckle of my middle finger.

"Mr. Thumb, you have a foreign object in your knuckle. Now that doesn't mean it's from France or anything, that just means it shouldn't be part of you!"

Sometimes doctor jokes were as lame as dad jokes.

Turning to Mom, Doctor Waggoner said, "I don't think it's infected, but as he moves his finger the bones will wear away on the graphite of the pencil tip and it could become infected. He should get that removed as soon as possible."

"How do you do that?" I asked.

"I don't do that Mr. Thumb, a hand surgeon does. Your mom will have to arrange to have a surgeon take that out."

Mom was sitting there just taking this all in. Doctor's office, X-ray, now soon to be hospital and hand surgery – this had turned out to be a very expensive and troublesome balloon.

Chapter Seventeen

Hoops

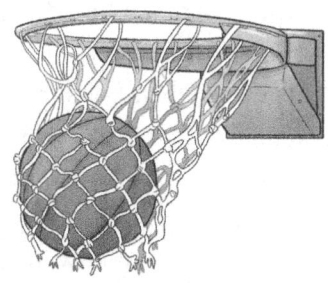

TWO DAYS AFTER SEEING Dr. Waggoner, I went to the hospital to have my finger operation. At each stop on the journey, I had to tell whomever was asking me how I got a chunk of lead stuck in my knuckle, and every time that I told the story, I got essentially the same reaction – a chuckling laugh accompanied by a back and forth head shake and some variation of "boys will be boys" said to me. I didn't see what the big deal was, and oddly enough, after a little while even I started to think that shooting myself in the finger was kinda funny instead of completely stupid. I guess that can happen when you tell a story often enough. As it was, I did get to spend the night in the hospital after the surgery, and that following morning I got to eat breakfast in bed! They even gave me one of those small cartons of chocolate milk, so it wasn't all bad.

Four weeks! Four weeks! That's how long I had to have that massive cast on my arm! I couldn't believe that I had to have a cast all the way up to my elbow for a knuckle injury, but I did, so I just had to make the best of it. Once the cast came off, then I had to have a splint on my finger for another three weeks!

Finally, the big day came when I was free of the splint, and I was back to normal. Well as normal as I could be! School had been pretty boring for me since I couldn't play any of the fun games at recess, and I hadn't been allowed to ride my bike with the cast on. But all of that was now in the past, and I was looking forward to trying out for our school basketball team.

My main friends at school were Tommy McHenry, Marty Collins, Steve Mozelli, and Nate Boehm. In school, the five of us were inseparable. Of the four of them, I got along best with Steve. He and I both liked messing around in the woods and fishing 'n stuff. However, since none of them lived in my neighborhood, or even within bike riding distance of our house, we really only ever saw each other at school. Us kids that went to St. Joseph's school came from several different neighborhoods around our town and as luck would have it, my friends were the most spread out. All of us that was, except for Tommy and Nate, cuz they lived right next door to each other. Therefore, we were all good friends in school, but overall, my best friend was my neighbor Dean who went to the town's public school.

Our basketball program started in sixth grade, so this was the first year that I could tryout. I liked basketball and we'd play either basketball or football during recess depending on what everyone wanted to do. I knew how to play, and most times, I could hold my own on the court. I just needed to hurry up and grow a few more inches before the season started. Unfortunately, with tryouts on Friday, unless I was going to sprout up that week, I would still be one of the shortest kids trying out.

Our best player was Tommy McHenry. During recess, when we picked teams he was always a captain. He was quick, had a great shot, and could dribble with either hand. Our recess games were always against the seventh graders since they had recess the same time as us. They usually always clobbered us in whatever game we played, but with Tommy and Nate who were our best players, we could sometimes keep it close. The good thing about our school's official basketball program was that we had separate sixth, seventh and eighth grade teams, so we didn't have to worry about trying to make the team against a bunch of older kids.

"Tommy are you looking forward to tryouts?"

"Auggie, I'm gonna smoke 'em! You know me; I don't even need to tryout."

Tommy definitely wasn't shy and sometimes was too cocky for my liking, but he could back it up with his play, and he was a better basketball player than me, so I left it alone.

Sure enough after tryouts, Tommy was our starting point guard, Nate and Joey Gionet were our starting forwards, Marty was our starting center, and Ryan Murphy was the other starting guard. Steve and I were the backups – me at guard and Steve at forward.

At school, I didn't hang around much with Murph and Joey G. It's not like we didn't like each other or anything, we all liked each other and we all got along swell, but they were in a different group of friends. When it comes to names, I don't think that I've ever met the person with the last name of Murphy who everyone didn't call "Murph," and Ryan was no exception. If it wasn't for the teachers calling out our full names when taking attendance, I probably would've gone through the entire year not knowing his first name was Ryan. As for Gionet, the "T" in his last name was silent. He said it was on account of it being a French name, and so everyone just called him Joey G. as if that was his first name.

During our first week of practice, our team started getting into synch as everyone learned their positions. Our first game was in a week, and we only had five more practices to prepare. Next week was going to be busy!

When it wasn't raining or snowing, my brothers and I would ride our bikes to school. It wasn't too far, just a few blocks past O'Malley Park so just a bit less than two miles away. That Monday morning as we rode up I saw a kid about my age that I didn't recognize. He was standing with a girl who I guessed must be his little sister.

"Hey, you new here?" I asked.

"Yeah, we just moved to town, and now we're going to school here."

"What grade are you in?"

"Sixth and my sister is in second."

"Cool, that's the same grade as me. My name's Auggie. What's yours?

"Brian, Brian Olson. What kinda name is Auggie?"

"It's short for August."

"It's short for idiot," my brother David said laughing as he and Timmy pushed by us.

"Don't mind them; they're just my moron brothers. If you want, you can follow me to Mrs. Duffy's class."

"Thanks, but I've gotta make sure that Lucy gets to her class, then I'll get there."

When I got to Mrs. Duffy's room, I found Tommy and the other guys and told them that we had a new student in our class. Just as I was finishing telling them about Brian, he walked in.

"All right children, please take your seats now. I have an important announcement."

Mrs. Duffy was a real grandmotherly type, and we figured that she had to be at least eighty years old or so. My dad told me that when he was a kid, she was his sixth grade teacher as well. Old she may be, but she was nice and never yelled at us. If we misbehaved, she just smiled and sent us to the principal's office. I much preferred just getting yelled at – because if you ended up in the principal's office that meant a note home to your parents and that meant a whole nuther level of trouble.

"Class, this is Brian Olson. He just moved here from Chicago, so let's take turns introducing ourselves to him." Pointing to the girl sitting in the first seat in the first row, Mrs. Duffy said, "Charlotte, why don't you start, please."

Brian sat in an open seat a few rows away from me. We all went around and said our names to him. There were twenty-five of us in sixth grade, well now there were twenty-six, counting Brian.

Once the introductions were finished, Mrs. Duffy started class and within a few minutes we were knee deep into spelling words and making sentences.

After what seemed like days, the lunch bell finally rang, and we all put away our books and lined up to head down to the cafeteria. For lunch we sat at these big long tables with the steel folding chairs. All of us boys sat at one of the tables, and all the girls sat at another table as far away from us as was physically possible.

"Brian, whaddya like to do? Do you play any sports?" Murph asked.

"I like hoops – basketball."

"We know what hoops are!" Tommy said kinda mockingly.

"We might be small town Iowa, but just because we ain't big city Chicago, that don't mean we can't ball."

I was taken aback by the edge to Tommy's voice, as I didn't think that Brian meant any harm by what he'd said.

Murph and Joey G. started talking to Brian, and then Tommy yelled for us to go shoot "hoops" before recess ended. We woofed down our food and Tommy, Nate, Steve, Marty and I all ran out. Brian, Murph and Joey G. hung back and sat there continuing to talk. Oh well, I'd catch up with them later. Besides, I was hoping to get some good basketball tips from Tommy.

After school, we all headed to the church hall that doubled as our gym. It had baskets at each end of the room but before we could start practice we had to put away all of the tables and chairs, sweep the floor, and get the balls out. As we were doing this, Brian walked into the hall along with Coach McClintock. Coach gave him a pat on the back and directed him to the men's bathroom, which was our "locker room" so he could change into his gym clothes. When he came out, Coach called us all together.

"Boys, I think that you've all met Brian today, and good news, he's joining our team! Please give him a big Tigers' welcome."

We didn't have any kind of official Tigers' welcome, coaches just said stuff like that to act like coaches so we just all said, "Hey Brian," and that was our Tiger's welcome.

"Form up into two lines, one behind Tommy, and the other behind Murph. Time for layup drills!" Coach bellowed.

Tommy's line had the ball, and Murph's line was the rebounding line. After you shot, you went to the back of the rebounding line and vice versa. Tommy took off towards the basket trying to dribble between his legs, obviously showboating, but unfortunately, he dribbled right into his leg causing him to trip and lose the ball. Coach blew his whistle at him.

"McHenry, keep it simple please!"

"Yes Coach," Tommy mumbled.

Brian was next. He dribbled effortlessly and made a perfect layup. As soon as he saw his ball go in the hoop he turned and hustled right to the back of the rebounding line without saying a word. He had a serious, focused look on his face. As practice continued, it quickly became patently obvious – Brian could really 'ball.' At the halfway point, Coach McClintock had Brian and Tommy switching off at point guard and Brian had no trouble running our plays, it was as if he'd been practicing them all week with us.

Tommy looked steamed. He didn't say anything, but I could tell that he was upset about something. After practice he, Nate and Marty just left without talking to anyone.

Practice was like that for the rest of the week. Brian and Tommy were splitting time at starting point guard, and as Brian learned the plays, he became more familiar with everyone, and seemed to have an easier time of it. After Friday's practice, Coach called us all together.

"Boys, great practice this afternoon! You're looking sharp. Tomorrow's game is here at ten o'clock. Get to bed early and get plenty of rest. We're playing St. Peter's and they're tough."

"Coach, what are our positions?" asked Tommy.

"Mr. McHenry, I'm still noodling that through right now, so I'll let everyone know in the morning."

With practice over, we all got changed and headed home.

I was excited. Even though I wasn't starting, I looked forward to the game. I always loved wearing the uniform and being part of the team with everyone. It was fun to play kids from different schools and see how we stacked up against them. Tomorrow morning couldn't come soon enough.

"Dad, let's go or we'll be late!" I called out.

"Relax Auggie, we've got plenty of time." Dad answered.

We were all going to the game. Timmy and David's eighth grade game was right after mine and Polly always came to cheer us on.

"Hey Auggie, should I bring Jake so that I can let go of him in the hall during your game?" Polly cracked herself up as she asked this.

"If only you could! Just not during our game!" Timmy added.

Dad said, "Nope, Jake stays here. So please take him out and then we'll put him in the kitchen."

We got to the hall in plenty of time. I changed into my uniform and then Coach McClintock called us all together to start warmups.

"Here's the positions for today's game, Brian, you're running the offense at point, Tommy, you're at guard two, Nate and Joey G. at forward, and Marty at center. Everyone else is on the bench to start. Let's go!"

We all went through our pregame drills, then when the ref blew his whistle we went back to the bench.

"Okay, starting five on the court. The rest of you take your seats," Coach said.

"Hey, good luck guys!" I called out.

Tommy's face was red. He just couldn't believe that he didn't have the ball and wasn't running the offense. Brian didn't seem to notice and once the game started, he did a great job. He got us four quick points on two baskets, and then he made a great pass to Joey G. who went in for a layup.

On defense, Brian stole the ball, passed it to Marty who passed it to Nate who made a bank shot, and just like that, we were up eight to nothing.

The other coach called a timeout, and in our huddle, Coach told Brian and Tommy that as soon as we get the ball back do a give-and-go play.

Our give-and-go play was for the point guard to pass to the center and cut behind him while the shooting guard crossed in front of the center who would then pass the ball to the shooting guard as he made his move. If the shooting guard didn't have a shot, he was to pass it to the point guard if possible, to set up another play.

Marty blocked the St. Peter's player's shot and kicked it out to Brian who brought the team down the floor. We set up. Brian raised three fingers for the give-and-go and quickly passed to Marty. Tommy made his move in front of Marty, got the ball, but was completely smothered by the defense. Brian moved out into the open so that Tommy could pass to him, but Tommy didn't pass. He ignored him and actually tried a shot! He was completely off balance and falling backwards as he shot. It didn't get anywhere near the rim and St. Peter's recovered.

When the first period ended, Coach put in Murph and Steve and sat Tommy and Nate.

I got in for most of the second and third periods. Coach was great at making sure everyone played, and I scored a basket, so I was thrilled! We won by twelve points, and the game was never even close. After the game, everyone crowded around Brian. He'd been our leading scorer, and he had the most assists.

"Brian, that was awesome! You Chicago boys really do play hoops!" I said.

Coach had us all huddle up and said, "That was a great game boys! You all did well. However, we do have some things to work on next week in practice. I'll see you all on Monday."

After the game everyone except Nate, Murph and me left, as we were the only ones with brothers playing in the eighth grade game.

"Brian's pretty good, isn't he?" I asked.

"Yeah, he's not bad, but I think that Coach should have let Tommy run the team at point," Nate remarked.

"I dunno, he didn't have any problem running the game and for all his points, he also spread the love around, as we all got shots – even me!" Murph said.

"Yeah, whatever. I just don't think that it was fair to Tommy." Nate said.

"I hear ya Nate, but like Coach says, we all gotta earn our spots, and nothing's guaranteed," I said.

Chapter Eighteen

Forced to Choose

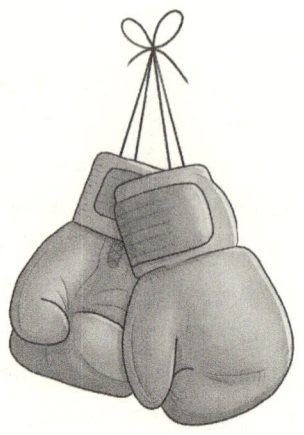

On Monday when I got to school I saw Tommy, Steve, Nate, and Marty all standing together outside the front door.

As I came up to them I called out, "Whazzup?"

"Tommy's gonna fight Brian on account of him stealing his position." Steve said.

"What? That's crazy!"

Tommy exploded, "No it's not. I don't know who he thinks he is coming in here and tricking Coach into giving him my position, but I'm gonna pound him."

"Tommy, I don't think he tricked anyone and besides you're still starting," I said trying to cool him down.

"Who ya for on this Auggie? You backing him over me?"

"I'm not backing anyone Tommy, I just think that you're nuts to fight him over this, and besides if you get caught, you'll be kicked off the team."

"No one's gonna catch us, we're doing it after school down the hill in the woods behind the gym. Besides, it'll be over in two seconds. I'm gonna flatten him with one punch."

"Guys, this is crazy!" I said.

"Auggie, you're either with us or against us, so you better decide." Nate said staring hard at me.

Before I could answer, the bell rang and we all headed inside. At lunch, I saw Nate go up and talk to Brian, and I could tell by the surprised look on his face that Brian had just learned he'd been called out.

When we all sat down at the lunch table it was me, Tommy, Nate, Marty and Steve at one end and Murph, Joey G. and Brian at the other. Tommy was talking real loud in our group and acting all stupid. He kept looking down the table at Brian and when Brian looked up, Tommy would punch his right hand into the palm of his left hand and put a tough look on his face. From what I could tell, Brian just ignored him.

I was not liking what I was seeing. However, these guys had been my friends ever since the second grade and I didn't want to lose them. On the other hand, I really liked Brian and as far as I could tell, he hadn't done anything to Tommy. He was just the better point guard.

The afternoon took forever to get over. Every time that I looked at the clock it seemed that the hands were turning backwards. Finally, it was two forty-five and school was over. Tommy immediately got up walked toward Brian, puffed out his chest and said, "You and me behind the gym, Olson."

Barely glancing up at him Brian replied, "If that's what you want, then okay."

Brian was completely calm and unfazed. I was beside myself. I liked both of these guys and didn't want to see them fight, but there was nothing that I could do to stop it. We all went out behind the gym and Tommy reminded everyone there that no matter what happened, if anyone said anything, he'd pound whoever told on him.

Tommy and Brian squared off and started circling each other.

"Tommy, we don't have to do this, ya know," Brian said coolly.

"Yeah we do, you stole my position and that ain't happening."

"I didn't steal anything," Brian answered.

Hoping to catch him off guard, Tommy didn't answer Brian and suddenly swung his right fist at Brian's chin, Brian blocked it up with his left arm and punched Tommy smack dab in the stomach. Tommy doubled over and let out a loud "huuumpff" sound as he fell backwards landing in a heap on the ground. He just sat there gasping for air and fighting back tears. Tommy didn't even make a move to get up. He was beat and he knew it. Brian meanwhile stood with both hands up and ready for whatever might happen next. He kept his eyes on Tommy until Nate suddenly stepped in.

"Okay, okay, it's over. You guys get out of here," Nate said.

Murph, Joey G. and Brian walked away. I could see that Brian was upset.

"That wasn't fair, he sucker punched me!" Tommy wailed.

"Yeah he sucker punched you," chimed in Steve and Marty.

Huh, sucker punch? Not hardly I thought, and then I said, "I didn't see a sucker punch, I mean you swung first, Tommy."

"The heck I did Thumb! Maybe you'd like to fight me," Tommy challenged.

"I don't want to fight anyone. I just want to play basketball."

"Well we're not liking Olson anymore. He can go be a loser by himself from now on."

"That's stupid." I said.

"Well if you want to hang around with us, then you can't be nice to him. You gotta hate him since he sucker punched me."

I couldn't believe it. I was being forced to pick who I could be nice to. I'd been with Tommy and these guys for so long, and I didn't want to lose them as friends. However, if this is what it took to hang around with them, then the choice was easy.

"Sorry guys, I'm not hating anybody, and Tommy, he didn't sucker punch you. He hit you fair and square."

I knew at that moment that I'd never be in their "crowd" again, but I also knew at that moment that I'd done the right thing. I turned around, picked up my gym bag and headed up the hill to practice. Breaking into a run I quickly caught up with Murph, Brian and Joey G.

"Hey guys, whazzup?"

Chapter Nineteen

"Whoa"

COACH NEVER DID FIND out about the fight, and afterwards our team did the best we could to regain our previous chemistry. However, it was never the same as before. In spite of that, we had a good run; winning more than we lost. We finished our season losing a close one in the semifinals of the conference tournament. But more importantly, I became good friends with Murph, Brian and Joey G.

I think that I also grew up a bit after Tommy and Brian's fight and that basketball season. I saw firsthand what Mom and Dad had always told me about the importance of good friendships and how a person's true character is revealed when things don't go his way. Seeing Tommy act like he did made me realize that I had wanted him for a friend for all the wrong reasons. I thought hanging out with those guys made me part of the "in" crowd and made me popular, but when I saw how easily Tommy could toss me aside, I realized that he wasn't a true friend. I have to admit that at first it hurt, but that feeling immediately evaporated the moment that I'd stood up for Brian.

"Hey Auggie, whaddya think Mom and Dad are getting us for our birthdays this year?" Timmy asked.

Since our birthdays were only one day apart, we always celebrated them together, and when you add in the fact that Christmas was less than two weeks after that, my birthday seemed more like a speed bump on the way to Christmas than a major event.

"I dunno, Timmy. I've been dropping hints for a shotgun so that I can go pheasant hunting with Uncle Alan and Uncle Howard, but I haven't gotten any commitment from either Mom or Dad. Heck, I still don't even have a BB gun."

"Yeah, but ya never know Auggie, maybe Dad will break down and get you one," Timmy said laughing at the sheer unlikeliness of that event ever actually even happening.

So, whaddya want for your birthday, Timmy?"

"I'm hoping for a Vikings' jersey or even a new bike."

"I definitely want a new bike," David chimed in. "I mean I'd still take a shotgun for my birthday, but I doubt if Mom would go for that, and besides, we still have a lot of work to do to train Jake."

"Yeah we do," I said. "I still can't believe that you guys would rather play football and basketball than go hunting. Ya know, Uncle Alan's been helping Dad and me with Jake and he's coming along pretty good. Uncle Alan says that he'll be ready for next season and that we can take him out with Nellie and Duke."

"Auggie, just wait until you get to junior high, you'll see how much fun football is." David said. "And besides, who knows, if it actually happens maybe I'll hunt with you some next year."

My brothers hadn't helped much in training Jake for hunting – they were too busy with their other stuff. I didn't mind so much, but while I would've appreciated the extra help, it did allow me to spend more time with Uncle Alan training Jake. Dad would help when he could, but now in the winter, when he got home from work, it was already dark. Uncle Alan worked different hours and came home earlier. Sometimes he'd come over to our house after he got off work, or I'd take Jake over there. Jake could sit, stay and come when called, but the command that a field dog really needs to know is "whoa" and that was what Uncle Alan was teaching me today.

When Jake and I got to their house, Uncle Alan was already home from work. After saying hi to Aunt Joan and playing with their kids for a bit, my uncle and I headed outside with Jake.

"Auggie, here's how you do it. We've gotta get Jake to immediately come to a stop the instant that he hears whoa."

We were outside in the backyard and Uncle Alan lifted Jake up and set him on the picnic table. He kept one hand in front of Jake on his chest, and used his other hand to hold the base of Jake's tail. Once Jake was steady, Uncle Alan gave him a treat and in a soothing reassuring voice repeatedly said "whoa" to him. He only did this for about a minute or two then he picked him up and set him down on the ground.

"Auggie, the goal here is to get him to stand still. You don't want him to sit down, that's why we keep a hand on his tail. This is the command that helps him when he points a bird. If he's allowed to sit on this command, then when the time comes, he might end up just sitting down when he smells a bird, and we don't want that to happen."

"Why do we set him on a table?"

"When he's on the table he's easier to control and he doesn't have anywhere to go. Keeping your hands on him lets him know that you're in control and makes him feel secure. Therefore, you have to be strong and steady. Here, you try it. We're only going to keep him on the table for a minute or so, just so you can give the command and get him to stay still. As soon as he stays still, give him a treat and then lift him down. Remember, if he's not getting it, it's not his fault, so you can't ever get mad at him. Instead think of what you should've done differently."

"Okay."

I bent down, picked up Jake and set him on the table. I wasn't nearly as good as Uncle Alan was, and Jake didn't want anything to do with the table, me, or whoa. My grip wasn't strong enough and Jake quickly jumped out of my hands and off the table.

"Well, ya got close Auggie! Let's do it again," Uncle Alan said chuckling. Then he added, "The secret to dog training is repetition, repetition, more repetition, and patience. The instant that it ceases being fun for you, it ceases being fun for the dog, and that's when you stop and go do something else."

"Yessir."

Uncle Alan helped me a few more times and finally I started to get the hang of it. Jake was getting the hang of it too, but Uncle Alan said this was the most difficult command to teach and it would take a long time to get it right. The table was also just the first part of the whoa training. Once Jake learned to stand still, the next thing was to train him on the move, then in a field, and finally with distractions.

"Ya know what Auggie? It's supper time, and besides that, I'm getting cold out here, so why don't you and Jake head home, and I'll head inside."

"Okay, thanks Uncle Alan! See ya later!"

Jake and I ran home, done with training for the day. I bounded up the stairs to the back door, pushed it open and Jake and I fell into the kitchen, letting all the cold December air in with us. Mom was at the stove getting our supper ready and as soon as those supper smells hit my nose, I realized how starved I was.

"August Thumb, don't just dump your stuff there! Boots off, and hat and coat on the hook please. Then get your dog fed, wash your hands and by that time, supper will be ready."

"Yes, Mom!"

After I put away my stuff and fed Jake, Mom called us all to supper.

"Hey Squirt, your birthday's in a few days ya know. How many balloons do you want Mom to get you?" Polly teased.

"Mom, no balloons for Auggie this year, right?" David added.

"I don't think that we can afford any more balloons, or pencils. The doctor bills are outta sight! Right my boy?" Dad asked grinning as he reached over and mussed up my hair.

"No, I'm good on balloons this year, but a nice twelve gauge shotgun, now that would surely work just fine," I replied.

"I don't think that you're old enough for those kinds of guns, August," Mom declared.

"Well how old were Uncle Alan and Uncle Howard when grandpa got them shotguns?" I asked.

"Well that's different," Mom answered.

"How's it different?"

"August, that'll be enough out of you!" Dad cut me off, as he didn't want me to put Mom on the spot.

"Sorry, Mom."

"Apology accepted, thank you, August."

We finished supper without any more talk about shotguns, and anyway I figured that there was no way I'd be getting one; Mom seemed to be absolutely dead set against it.

I kept training Jake and slowly he started getting the idea of whoa. We had mastered the table and we were now working on it in the backyard. Dad came out, gave me some pointers and tried it a few times with Jake as well. But then Mom called him inside to help her with something, and it was just Jake and me by ourselves.

As Jake moved around the yard sniffing stuff and looking for things, I would periodically call, "whoa" and see how he reacted. If he didn't stop, which he hadn't done yet, I'd come up to him, pick him up, carry him back to where he was when I had originally commanded whoa, set him down on the ground, and with one hand under his chin and the other holding his tail out say, "whoa." After several days of doing this, one afternoon when we were out in the backyard I waited until Jake was about twenty feet away from me and then I called, "whoa."

Jake came to a stop. An abrupt stop. A real perfect standing on all fours straight up stop. He stood there and looked right at me with his tail pointed up in the air!

"Jake, good boy! Good boy Jake!" I shouted with my heart just bursting out of my chest with shocked amazement.

I called him over to me and gave him a treat and all kinds of hugs and pets and he wiggled in excitement, his tail wagging a mile a minute. I was thrilled! I couldn't wait to show everyone, especially Dad and Uncle Alan, but before I'd show anyone I had to make sure that he really had it. Therefore, I released Jake and then as soon as he was a few yards away from me, I commanded "whoa" and once again he abruptly came to a stop. This was awesome! More treats, hugs and pets, and then we did it two more times, each time Jake coming right to a stop. He definitely had it down! I ran up to our patio door, opened it, stuck my head in, and called out to whoever was in listening distance, "Hey guys, come out here and watch what Jake can do!"

Mom and my brothers were the only ones home but they came to the back door to watch. Jake was running along the back fence and I called out, "whoa!" He stopped on a dime and looked right at me!

"Well done! August, that's great!" Mom exclaimed.

"Yeah, well done little brother!" Timmy said.

"Maybe he'll be a hunting dog after all," David added.

"Thanks! He's a smart dog!" I replied.

"It's getting dark and it's time for you to come in and get started on your homework before dinner, Mom said.

"Will do, Mom. I just gotta put Jake's stuff away."

Tomorrow was my birthday. I was glad to be turning twelve, but now that Jake was learning hunting commands, I wished I could get a shotgun, but if not, I'd even be happy with a BB gun.

"Wake up Birthday Boy!" Dad called as he shook me awake. "Time to get up and get your day started!"

"Dad, it's 6:30 in the morning, and it's Saturday! This is my day to sleep in!"

"Well you can go back to sleep if you want to, but then when your uncles get here, I'll just tell them that you didn't want to go pheasant hunting with us."

"What? Huh? Wait, are you serious? How can I go pheasant hunting when I don't even have a gun?"

"Well Auggie, your mom and I talked last night. I told her how I was ten when I got my first gun, and I reminded her that her brothers were also ten when they started hunting, so the way I figured it, you were already two years late. It took a bit of convincing, but here's the deal. You are going to walk along with your uncles and me today and you're going to learn how to hunt. You won't be carrying a gun, but we'll teach you what you need to know to hunt pheasants, and afterwards you and I will go down to Harry's Gun Shop and get you a shotgun for your birthday!"

For a brief second, I was speechless.

"Really Dad, really?"

"Yep, really Auggie, and happy birthday, son!"

I gave my dad a big hug, jumped out of bed and quickly threw on jeans and a sweatshirt.

"Oh, Dad, as long as we're on the subject of buying guns, now that I've got enough money saved up, when we get to Harry's, can I buy that BB gun I've been wanting?"

"Ya know Auggie..., yes you can!"

About the author

The J in J.A. stands for Jim, and when Jim was a boy he grew up in an Iowa neighborhood that was just a stone's throw from woods and cricks, cornfields and farm ponds. Without any hesitation, Jim's parents swept him and his siblings outside every chance they could. Hiking through the woods, fishing and swimming in ponds, wrestling with his brothers, and playing hours and hours of backyard football and baseball shaped his youth. When it was time to be inside, reading was Jim's passion. He devoured every book that he could get his hands on. He now lives in Vermont with his lovely wife Darlene and after having raised four wonderful adventurous children, they are anxiously awaiting the birth of their grandchildren who will be sure to hear all about the adventures of Auggie Thumb. Check back often as Auggie will soon be experiencing more adventures.

Made in United States
North Haven, CT
15 April 2024